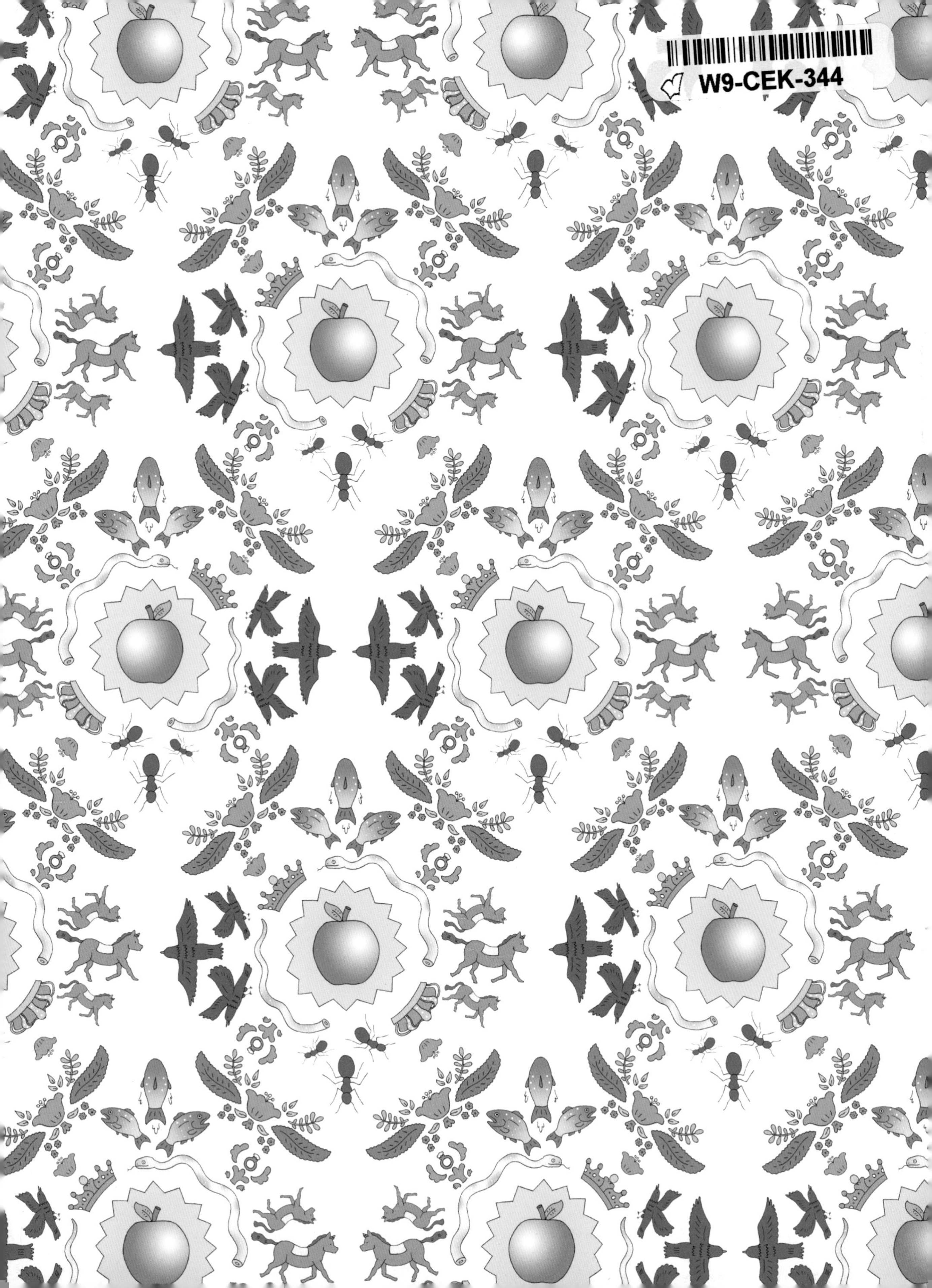

**For my mom, Jane**

*Walter Crane, pen-and-ink drawings for the 1886 edition of Household Stories from the Collection of the Brothers Grimm*

# The White Snake

A TOON GRAPHIC BY

**BEN NADLER**

*Based on a fairy tale by the Grimm Brothers*

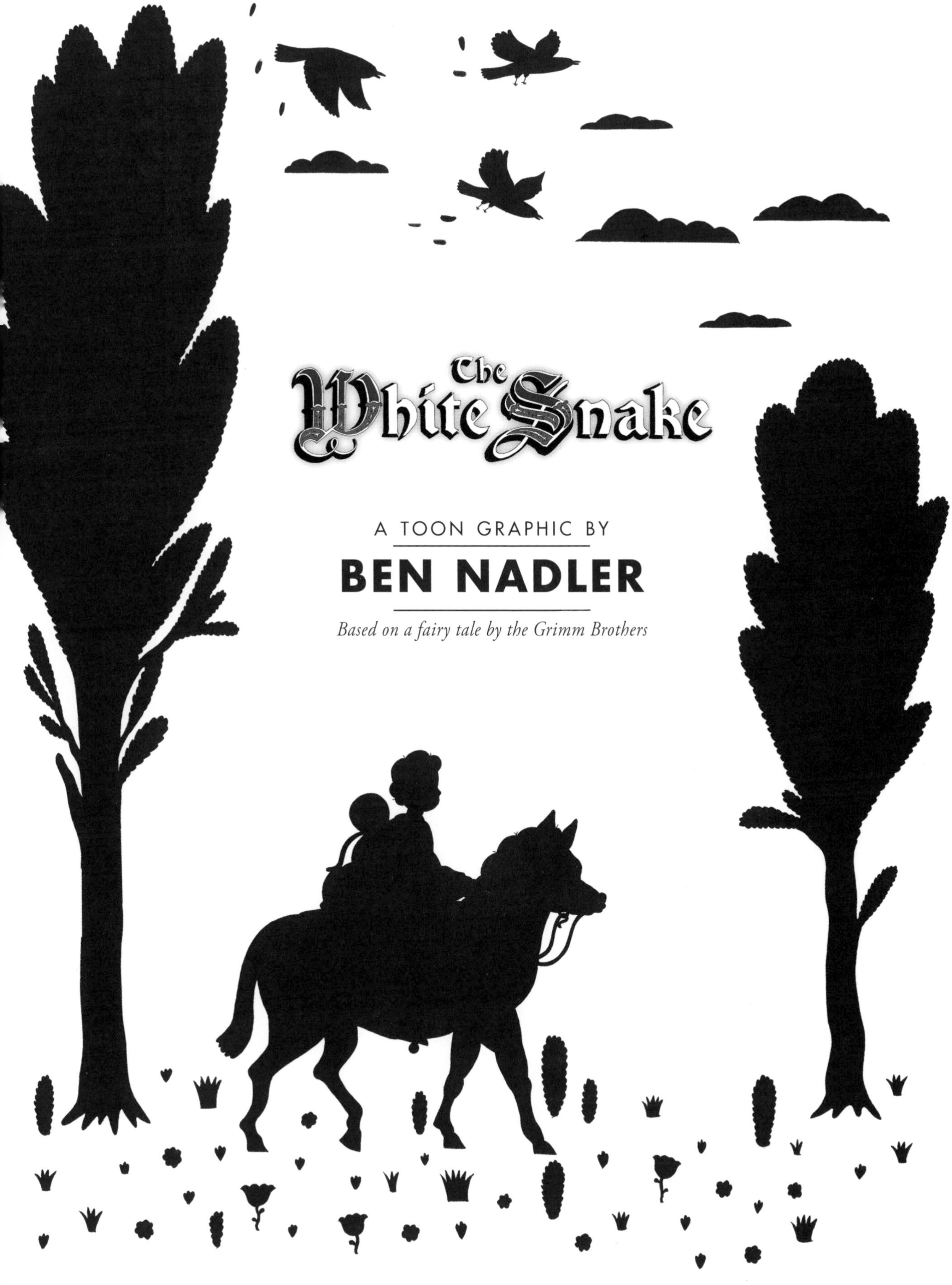

Editorial Director & Book Design: FRANÇOISE MOULY

Editor: PAUL KARASIK

Guest Editor: DASHIELL SPIEGELMAN

BEN NADLER'S artwork was drawn with India Ink on Bristol board and colored digitally.

FOR VISUAL READERS
TOON
GRAPHICS

A TOON Graphic™ © 2019 Ben Nadler & TOON Books, an imprint of RAW Junior, LLC, 27 Greene Street, New York, NY 10013. TOON Books® and TOON Graphics™ are trademarks of RAW Junior, LLC. All rights reserved. No part of this book may be used or reproduced in any manner whatsoever without written permission except in the case of brief quotations embodied in critical articles and reviews. Library of Congress Cataloging-in-Publication Data: Names: Nadler, Ben, adapter, artist. | Grimm, Jacob, 1785-1863. | Grimm, Wilhelm, 1786-1859. Title: The white snake : adapted from a fairy tale by the Grimm brothers / by Ben Nadler; with an afterword by Paul Karasik. Other titles: Weisse Schlange. English. Description: New York, NY : Toon Books, [2019] | Summary: A graphic novel adaptation of the tale of Randall, a young servant who eats a forbidden food, gains the ability to understand animals' speech, and attains great rewards. Identifiers: LCCN 2018040601 | Subjects: LCSH: Graphic novels. | CYAC: Graphic novels. | Human-animal communication--Fiction. | Household servants--Fiction. | Kings, queens, rulers, etc.--Fiction. | Fairy tales. Classification: LCC PZ7.7.N22 Whi 2019 | DDC 741.5/973--dc23 All our books are Smyth Sewn (the highest library-quality binding available) and printed with soy-based inks on acid-free, woodfree paper harvested from responsible sources. Printed in China by C&C Offset Printing Co., Ltd. Distributed to the trade by Consortium Book Sales & Distribution, a division of Ingram Content Group; orders (866) 400-5351; ips@ingramcontent.com; www.cbsd.com.

ISBN 978-1-943145-37-9 (hardcover)    ISBN 978-1-943145-38-6 (softcover)

19  20  21  22  23  24  C&C  10 9 8 7 6 5 4 3 2 1

WWW.TOON-BOOKS.COM

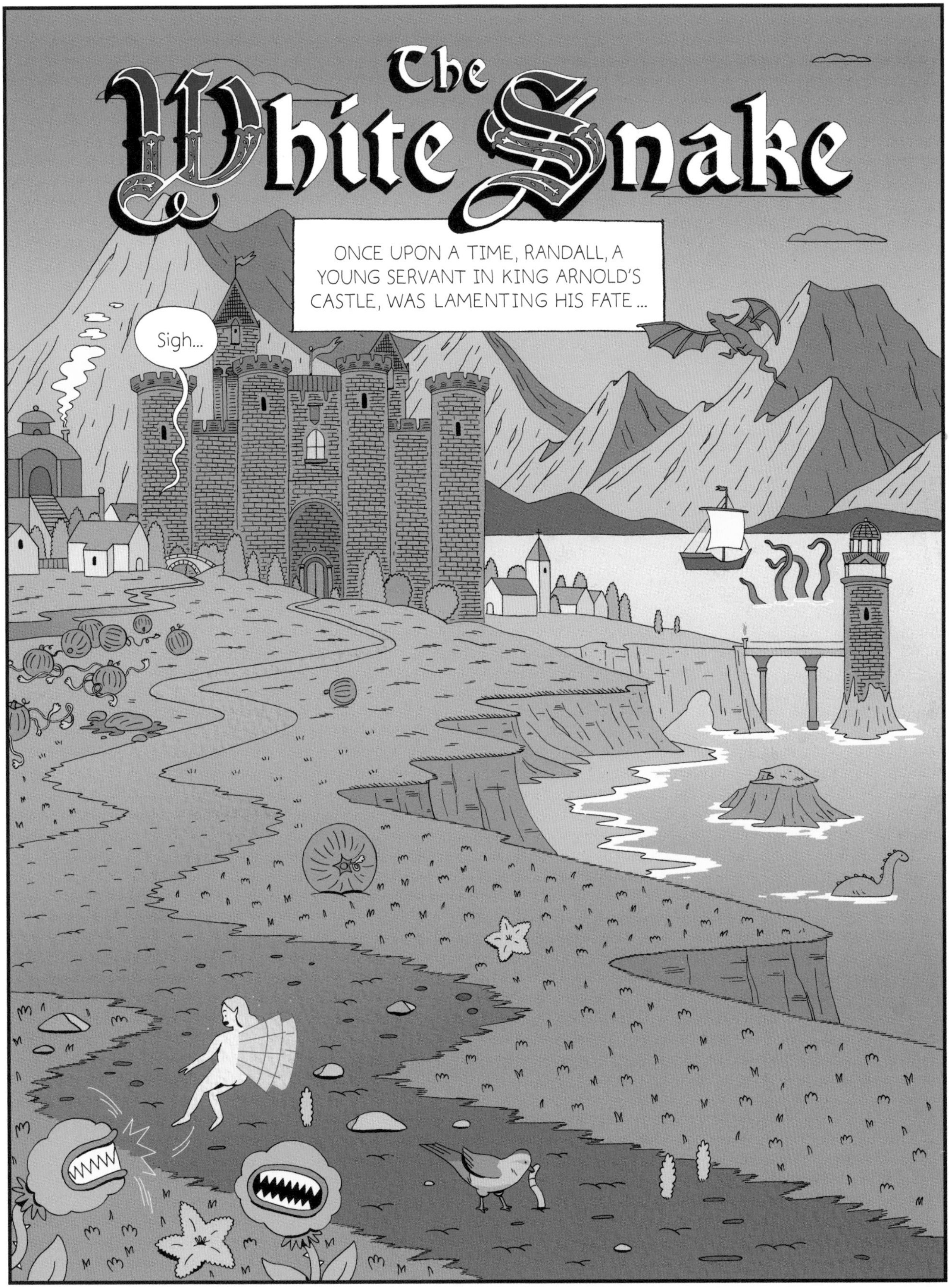
The White Snake
ONCE UPON A TIME, RANDALL, A YOUNG SERVANT IN KING ARNOLD'S CASTLE, WAS LAMENTING HIS FATE ...
Sigh...

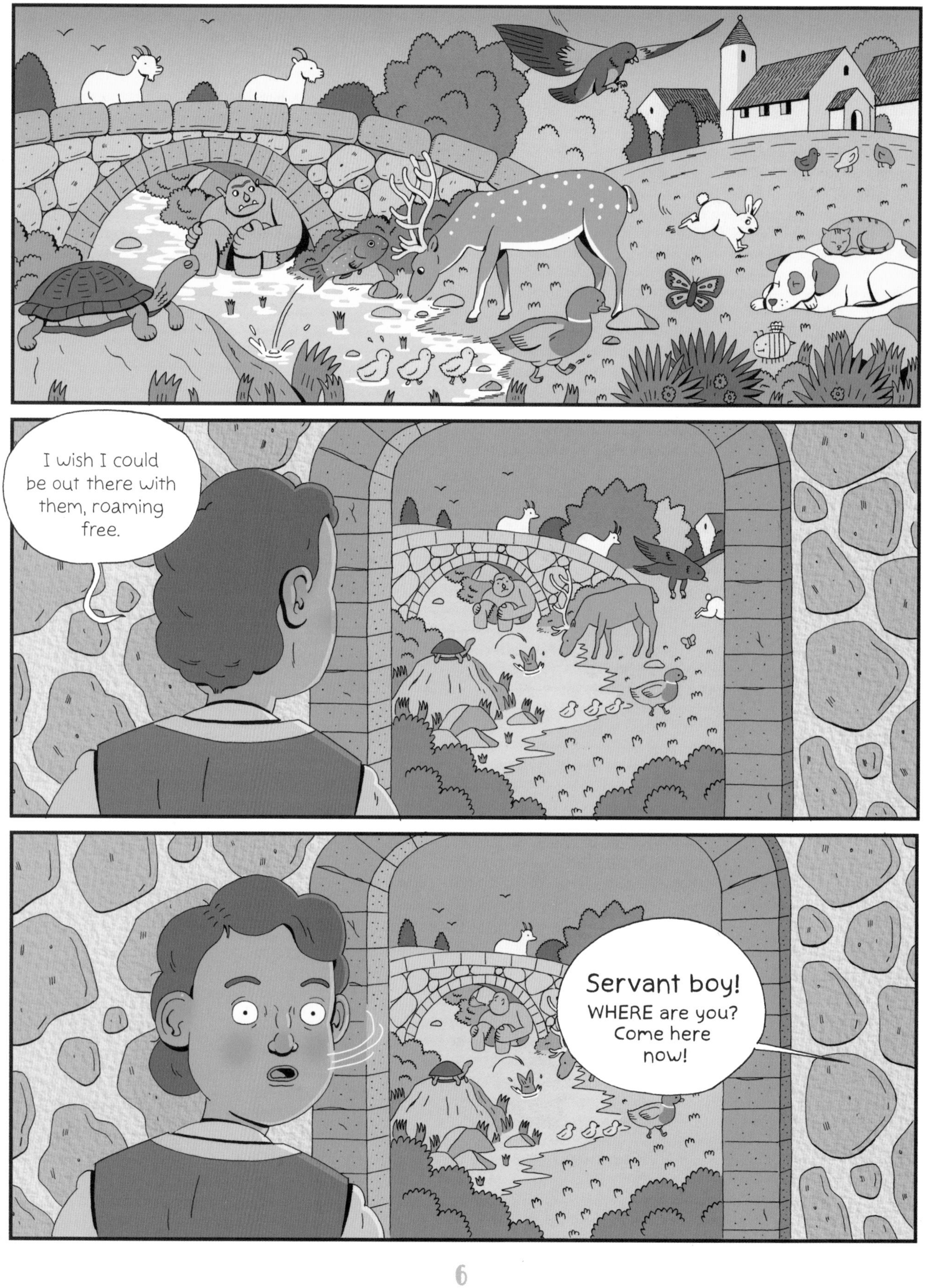
I wish I could be out there with them, roaming free.
Servant boy! WHERE are you? Come here now!

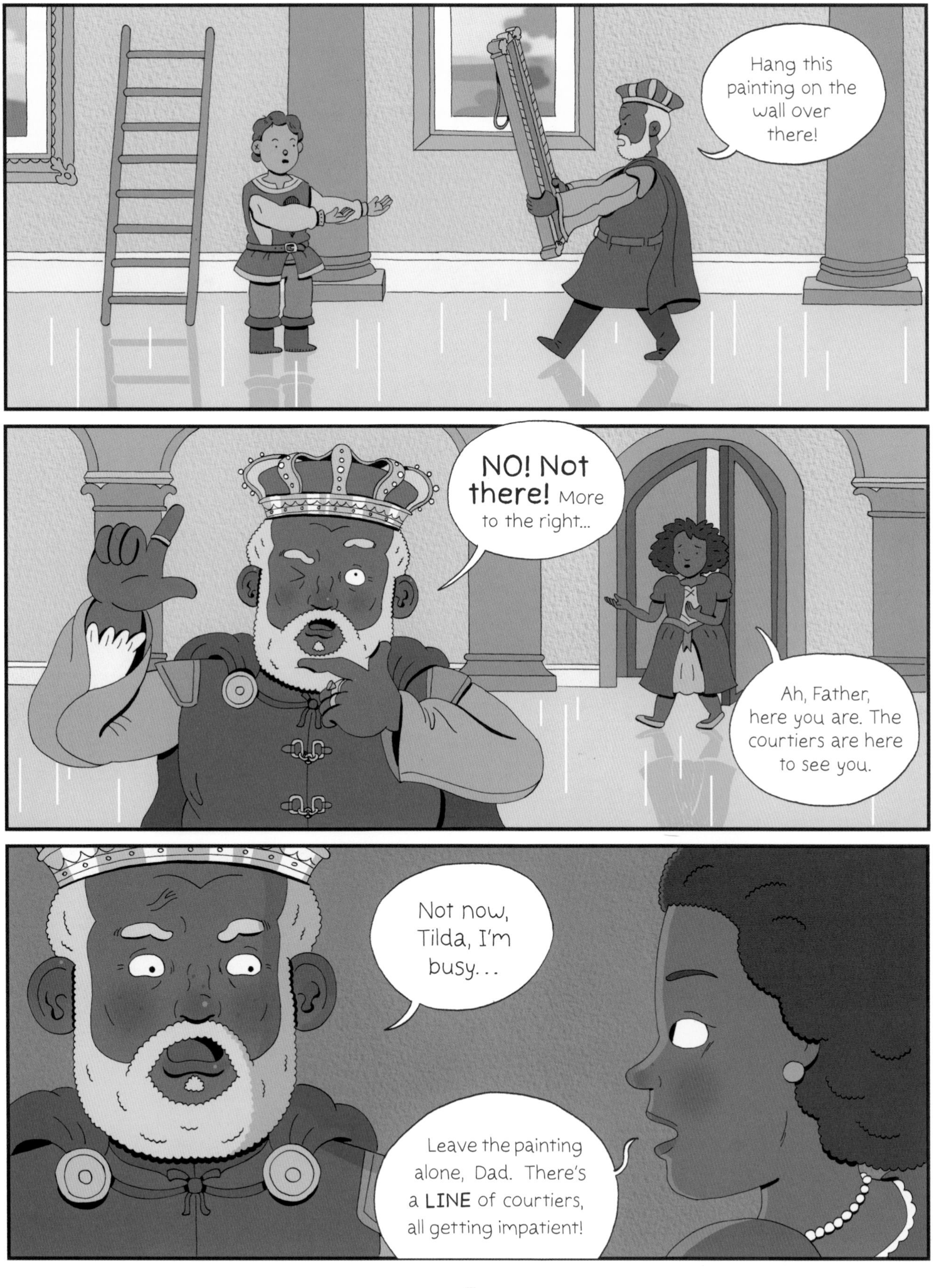
Hang this painting on the wall over there!
NO! Not there! More to the right...
Ah, Father, here you are. The courtiers are here to see you.
Not now, Tilda, I'm busy...
Leave the painting alone, Dad. There's a LINE of courtiers, all getting impatient!

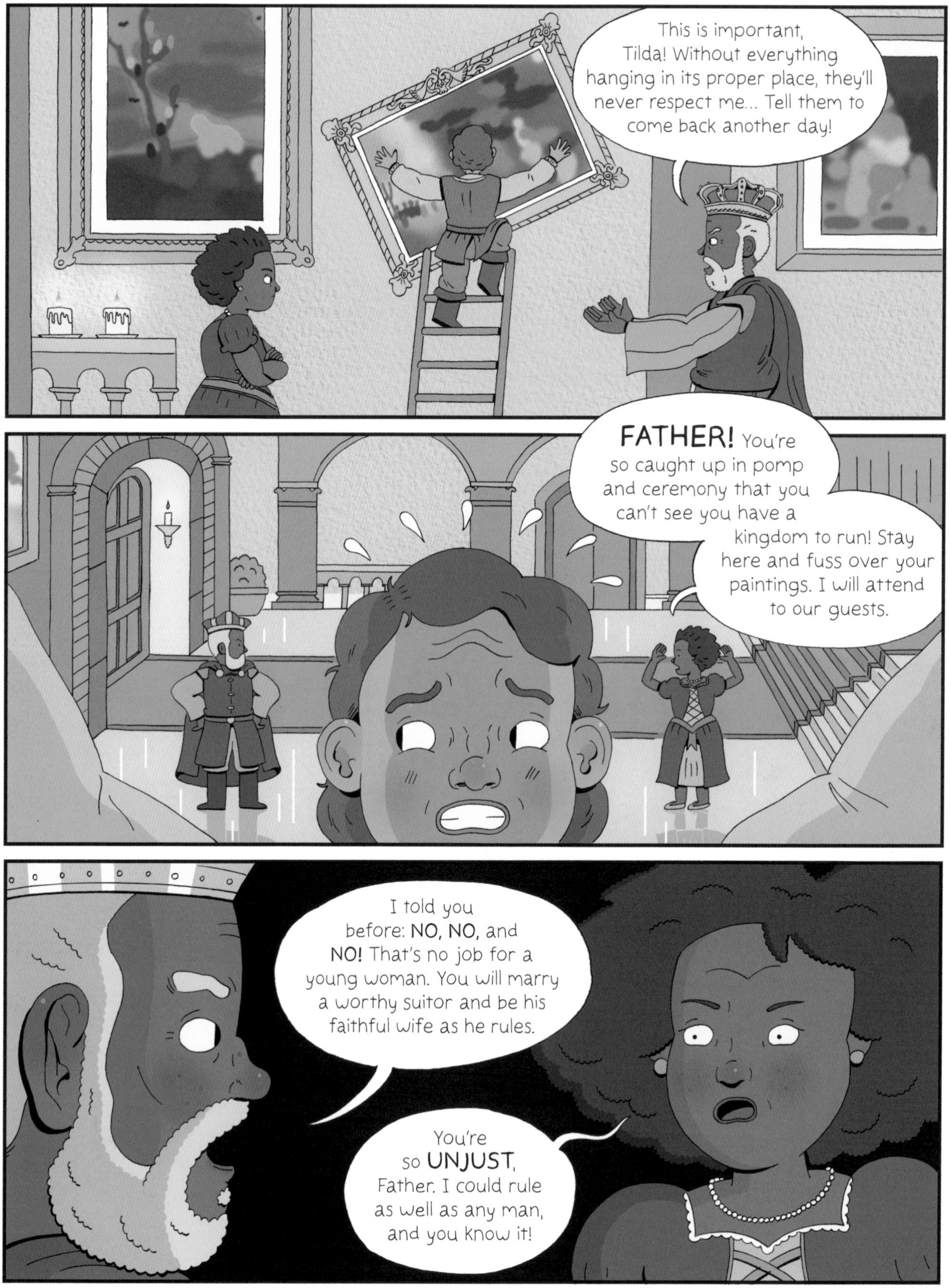
This is important, Tilda! Without everything hanging in its proper place, they'll never respect me... Tell them to come back another day!
FATHER! You're so caught up in pomp and ceremony that you can't see you have a kingdom to run! Stay here and fuss over your paintings. I will attend to our guests.
I told you before: NO, NO, and NO! That's no job for a young woman. You will marry a worthy suitor and be his faithful wife as he rules.
You're so UNJUST, Father. I could rule as well as any man, and you know it!

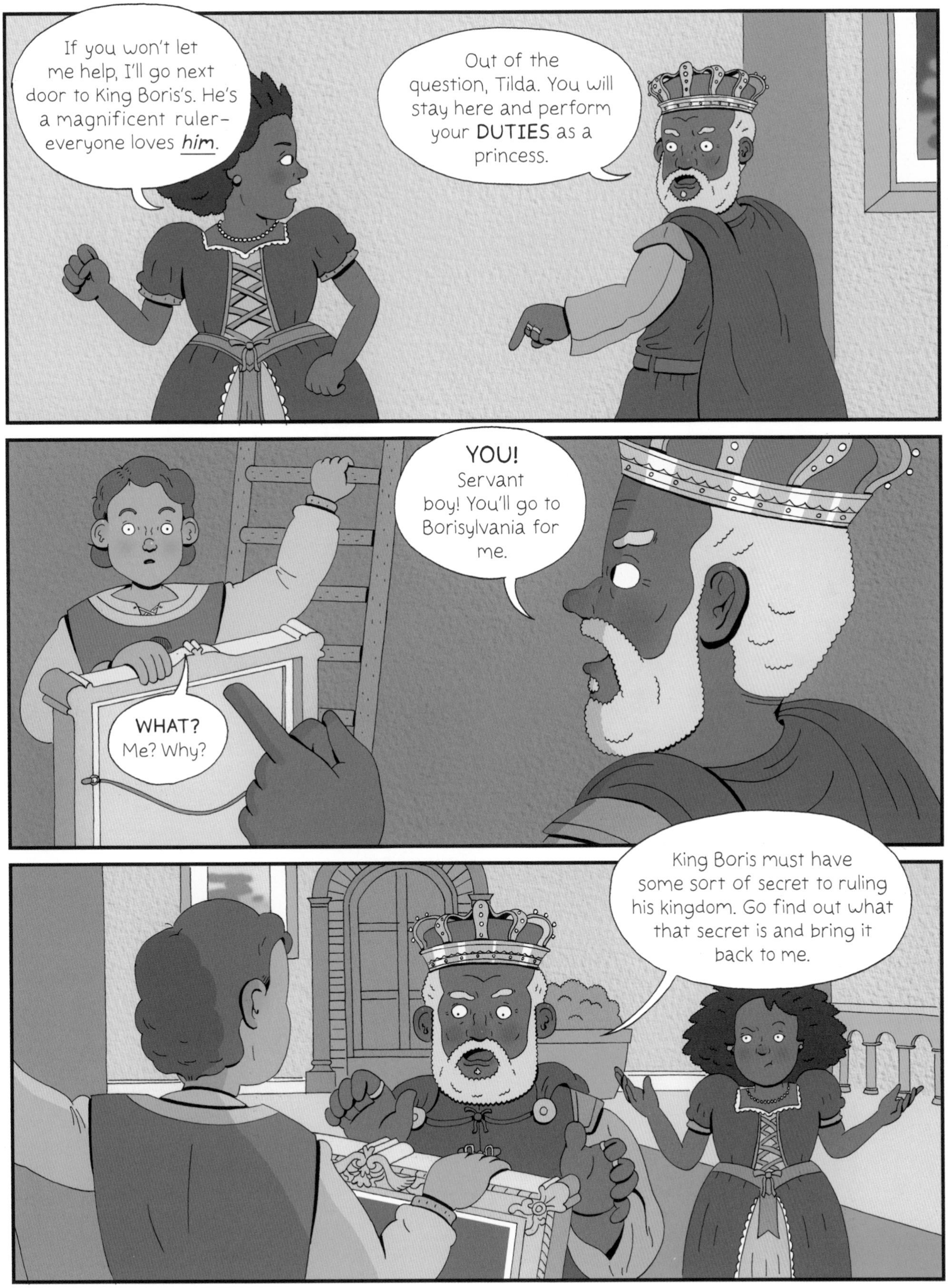
If you won't let me help, I'll go next door to King Boris's. He's a magnificent ruler– everyone loves him.
Out of the question, Tilda. You will stay here and perform your DUTIES as a princess.
YOU! Servant boy! You'll go to Borisylvania for me.
WHAT? Me? Why?
King Boris must have some sort of secret to ruling his kingdom. Go find out what that secret is and bring it back to me.

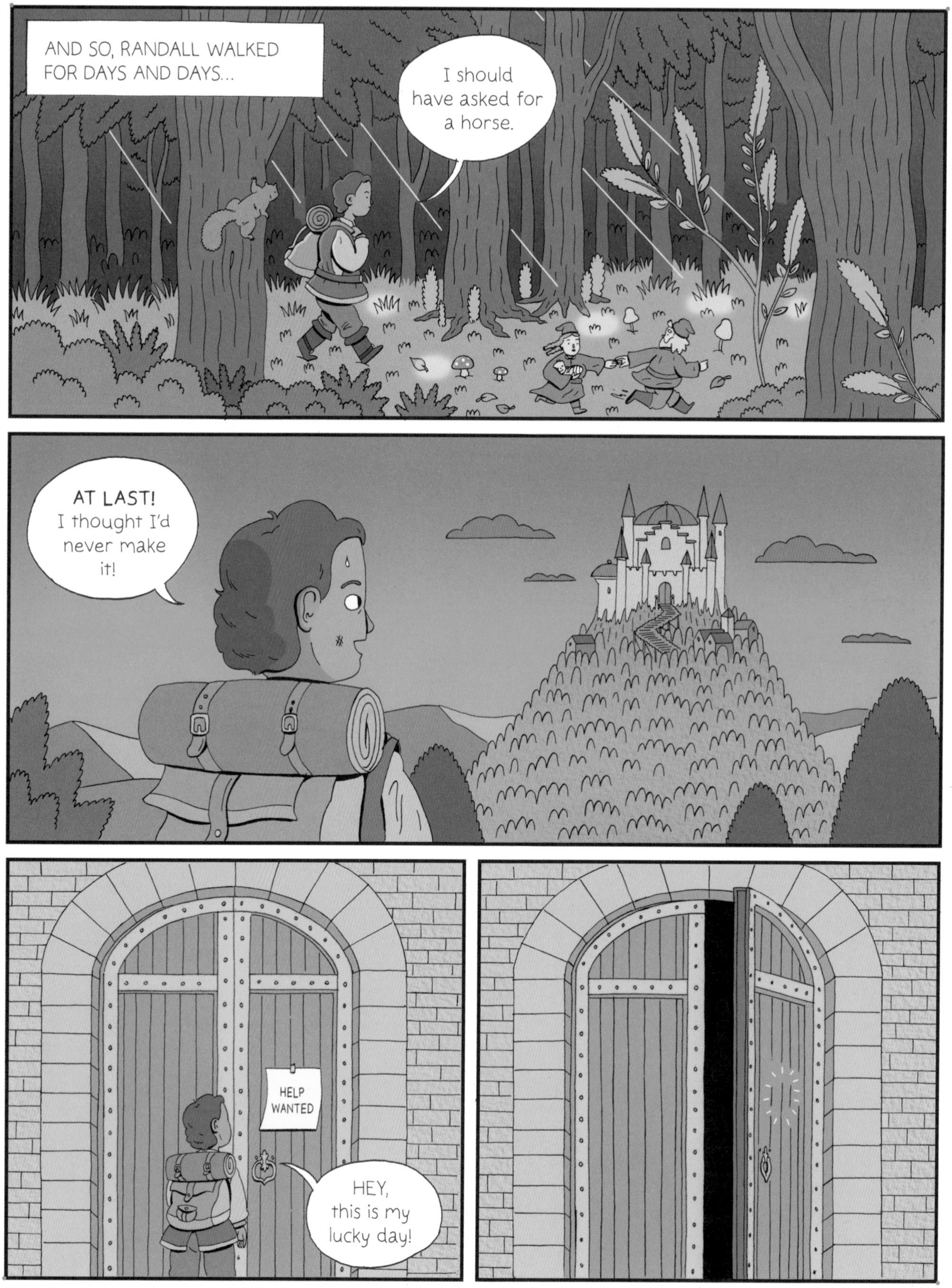
AND SO, RANDALL WALKED FOR DAYS AND DAYS...
I should have asked for a horse.
AT LAST! I thought I'd never make it!
HELP WANTED
HEY, this is my lucky day!

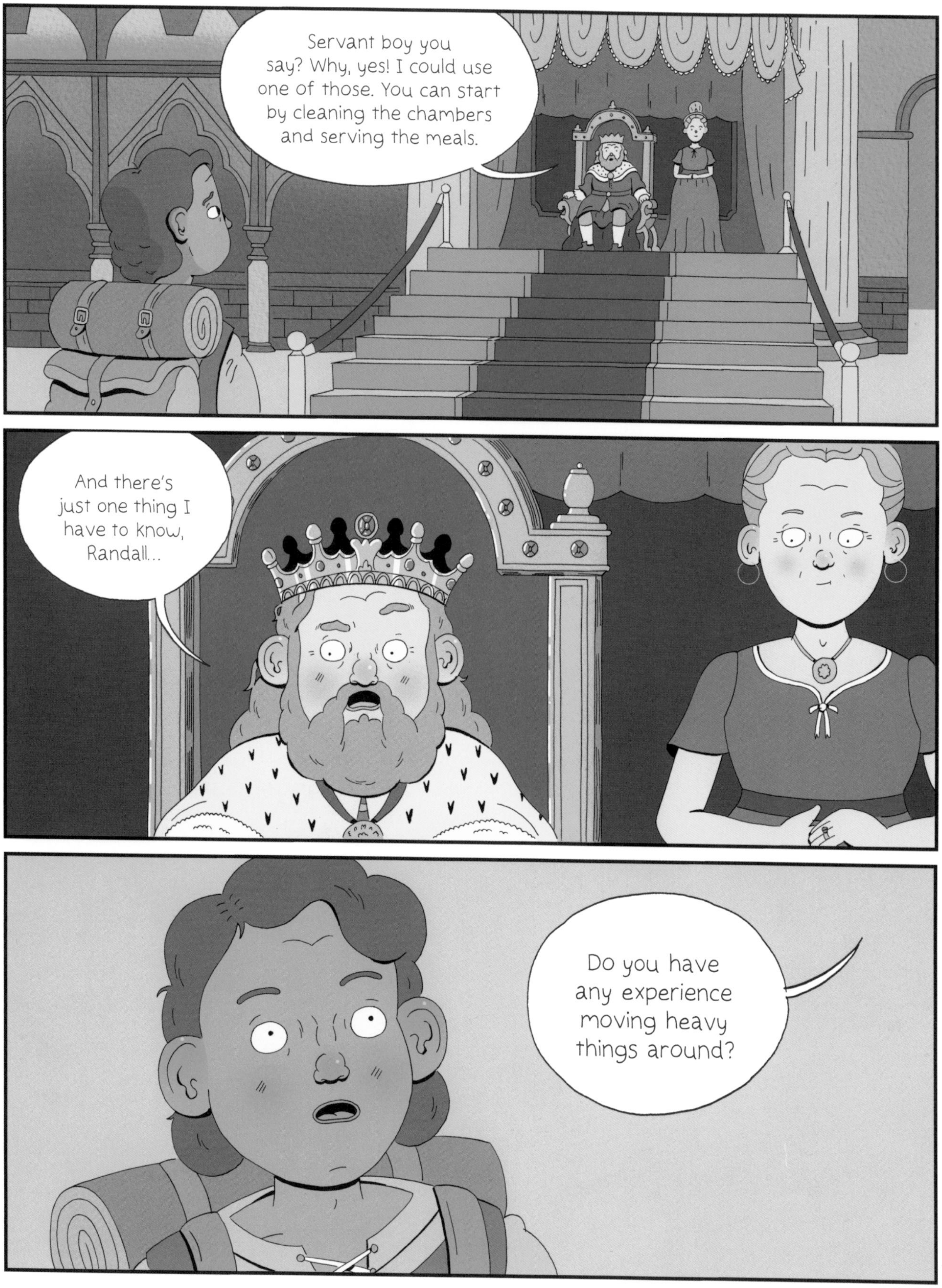
Servant boy you say? Why, yes! I could use one of those. You can start by cleaning the chambers and serving the meals.
And there's just one thing I have to know, Randall...
Do you have any experience moving heavy things around?

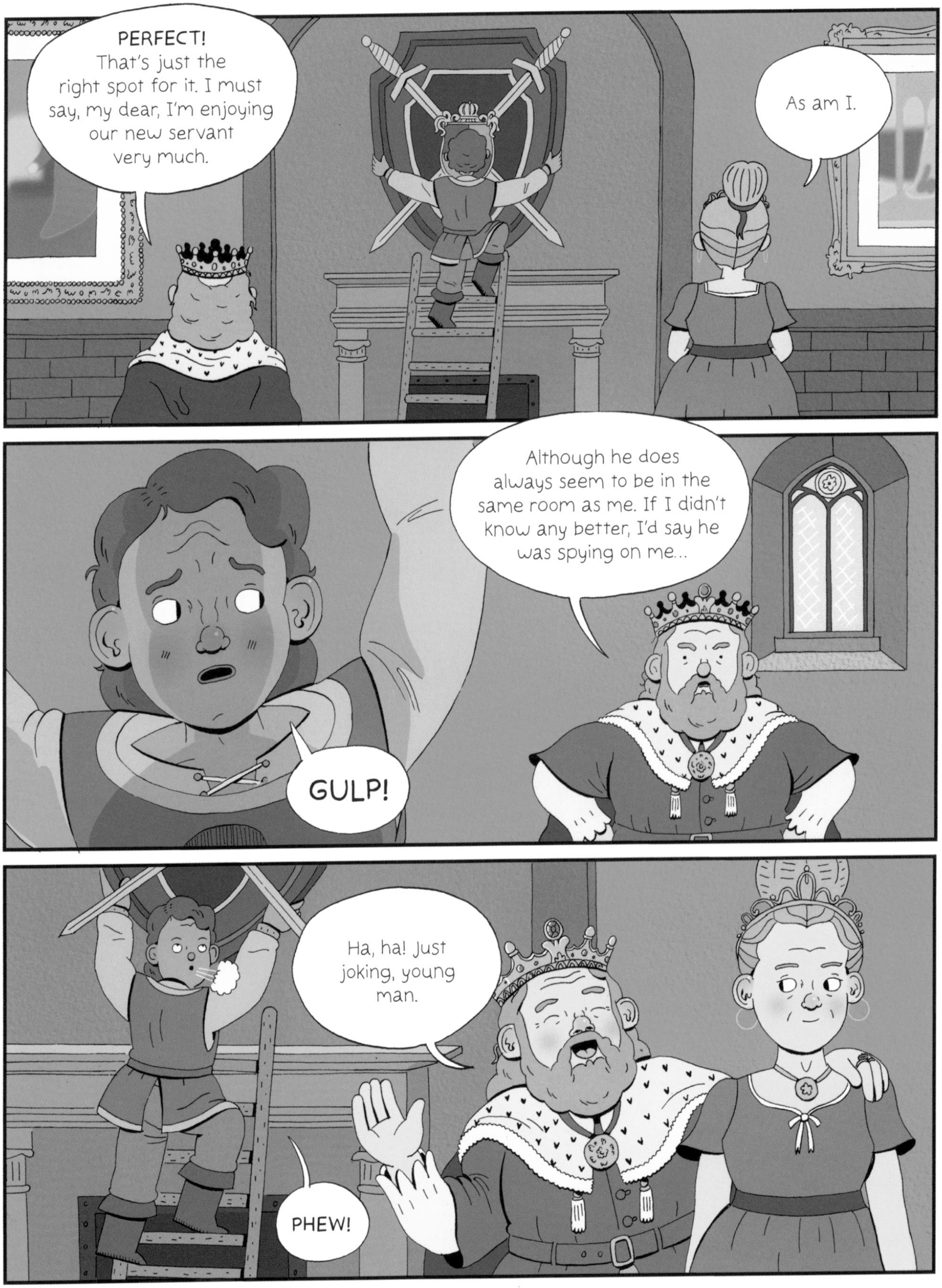
PERFECT! That's just the right spot for it. I must say, my dear, I'm enjoying our new servant very much.
As am I.
Although he does always seem to be in the same room as me. If I didn't know any better, I'd say he was spying on me...
GULP!
Ha, ha! Just joking, young man.
PHEW!

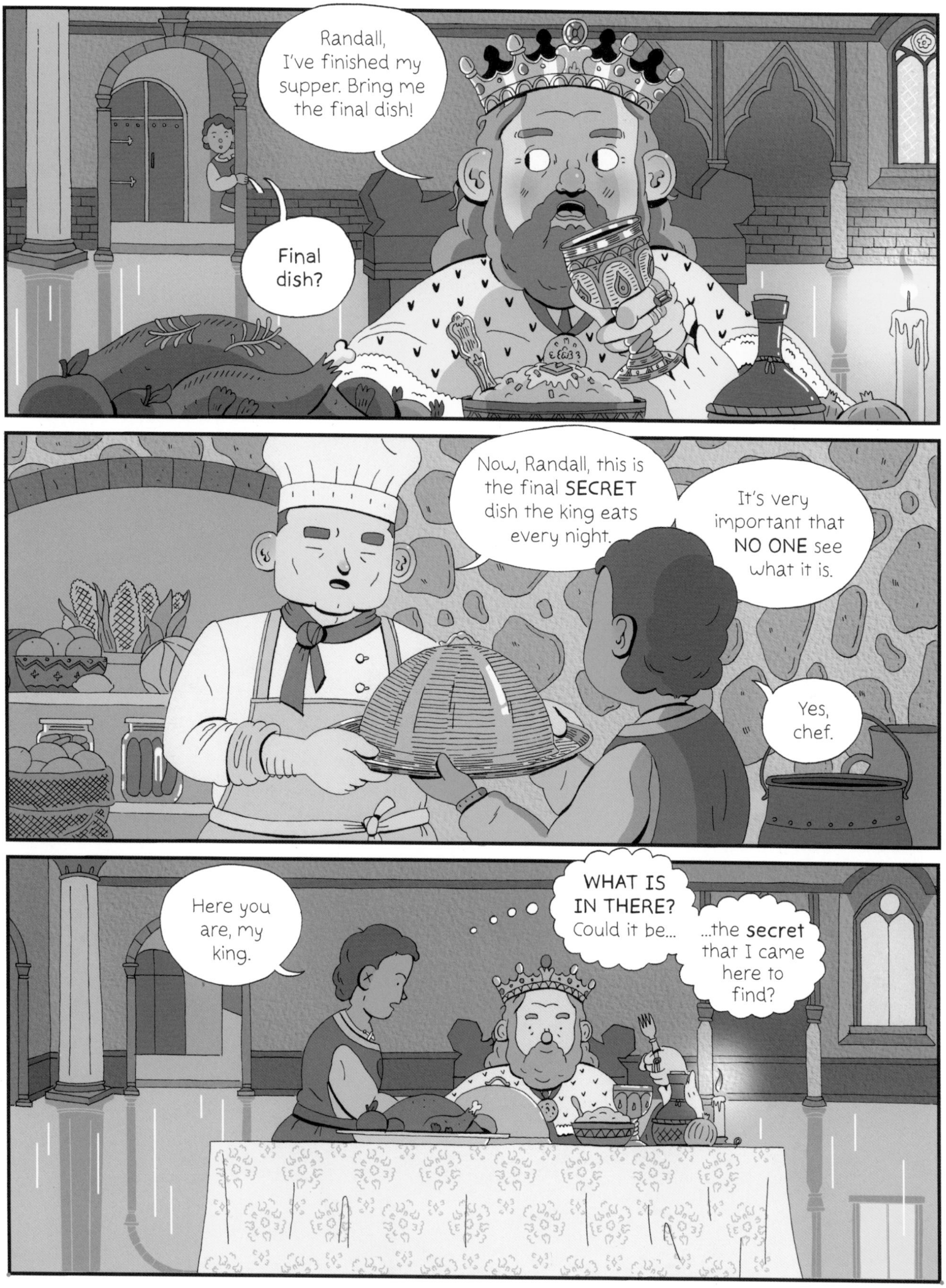
Randall, I've finished my supper. Bring me the final dish!
Final dish?
Now, Randall, this is the final SECRET dish the king eats every night.
It's very important that NO ONE see what it is.
Yes, chef.
Here you are, my king.
WHAT IS IN THERE? Could it be...
...the secret that I came here to find?

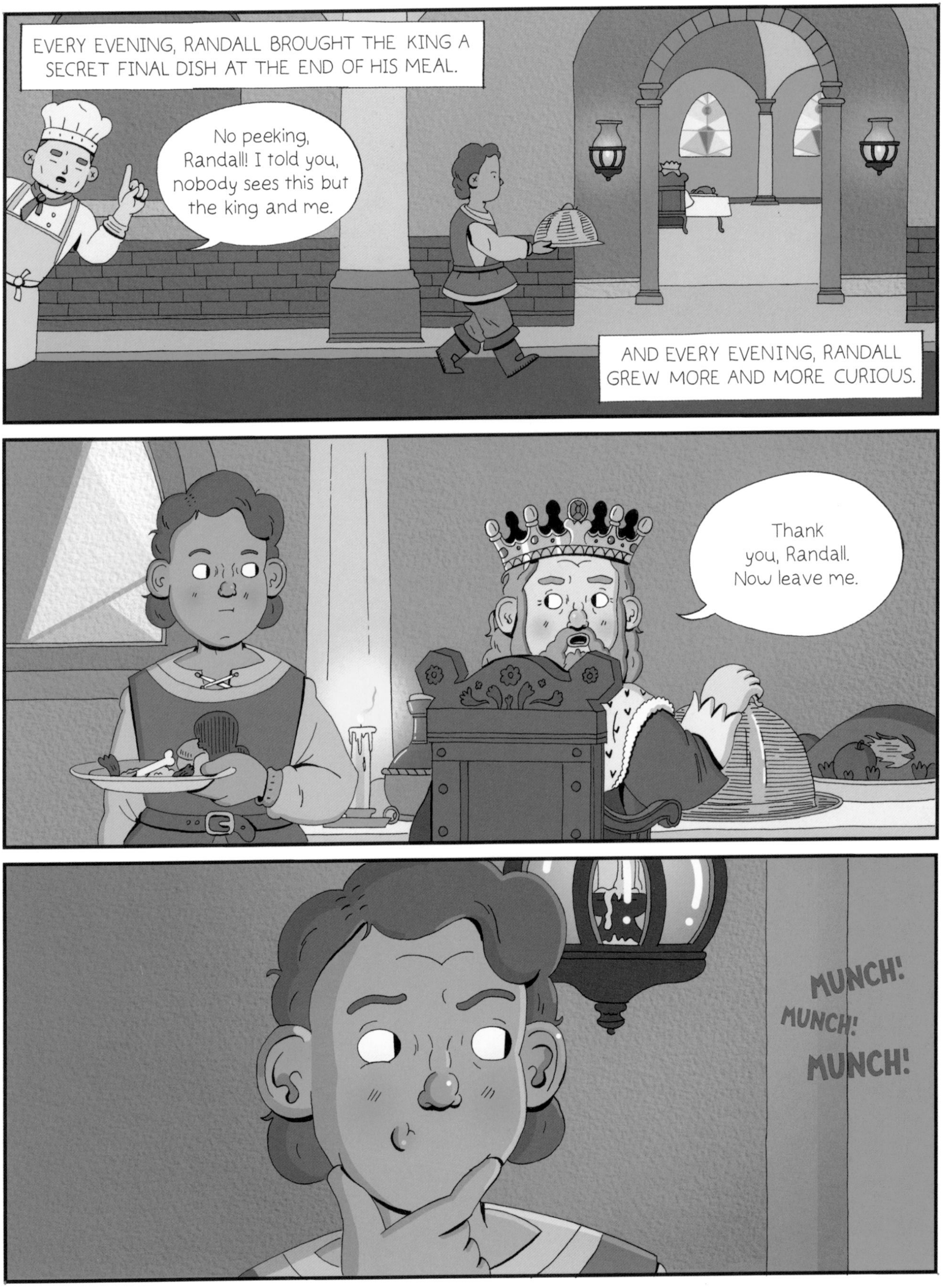
EVERY EVENING, RANDALL BROUGHT THE KING A SECRET FINAL DISH AT THE END OF HIS MEAL.
No peeking, Randall! I told you, nobody sees this but the king and me.
AND EVERY EVENING, RANDALL GREW MORE AND MORE CURIOUS.
Thank you, Randall. Now leave me.
MUNCH!
MUNCH!
MUNCH!

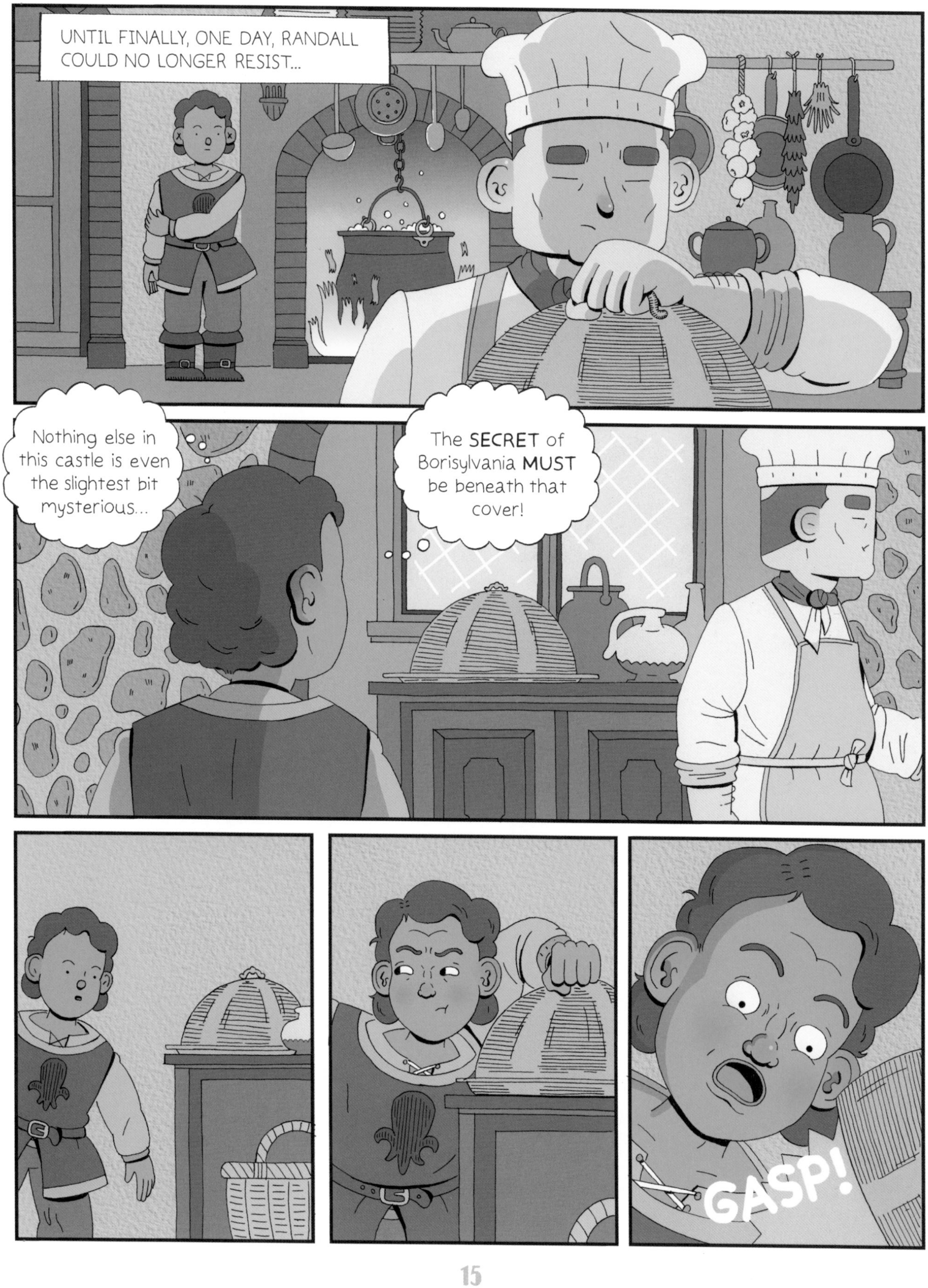
UNTIL FINALLY, ONE DAY, RANDALL COULD NO LONGER RESIST...
Nothing else in this castle is even the slightest bit mysterious...
The SECRET of Borisylvania MUST be beneath that cover!
GASP!

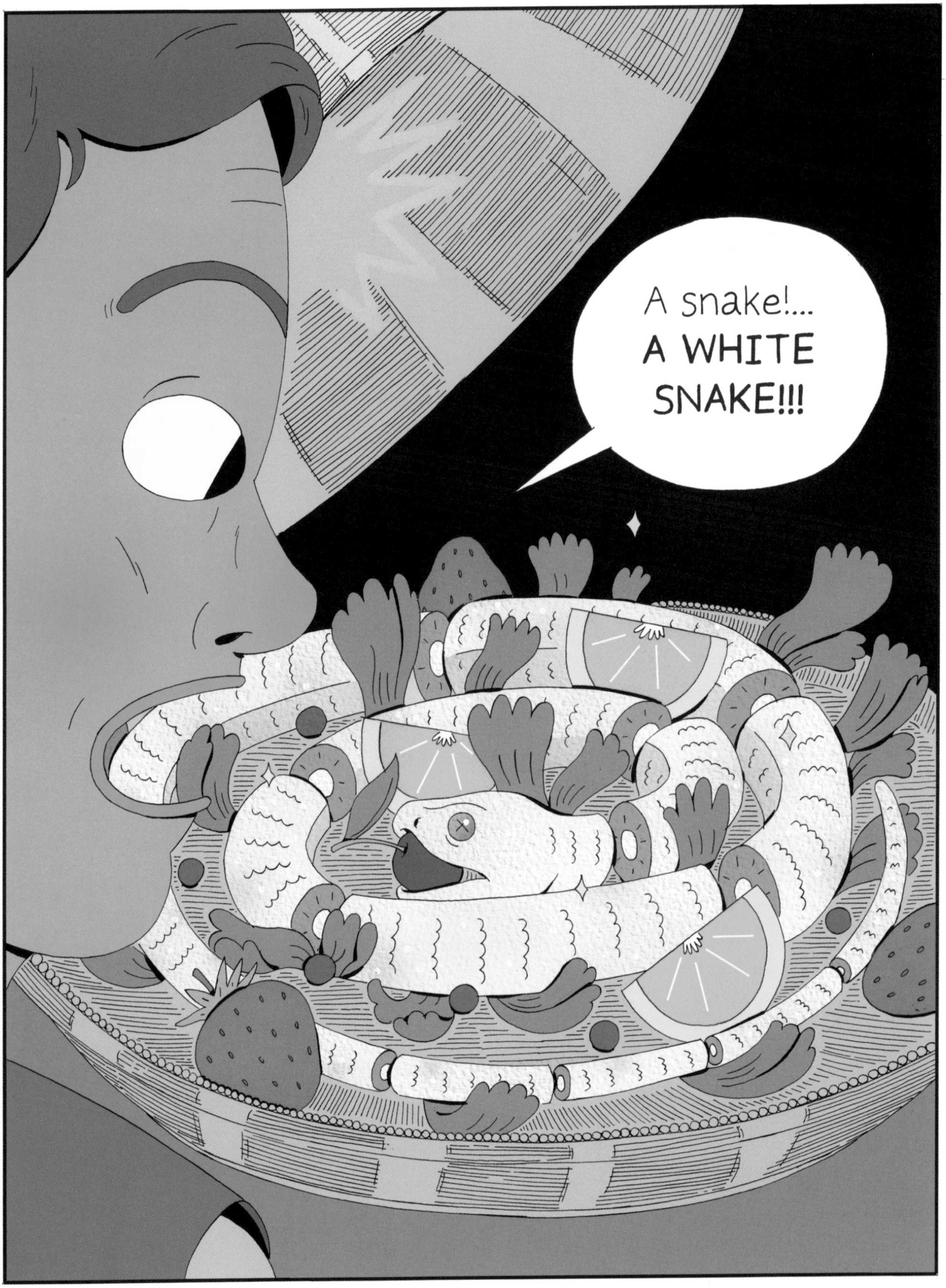
A snake!... A WHITE SNAKE!!!

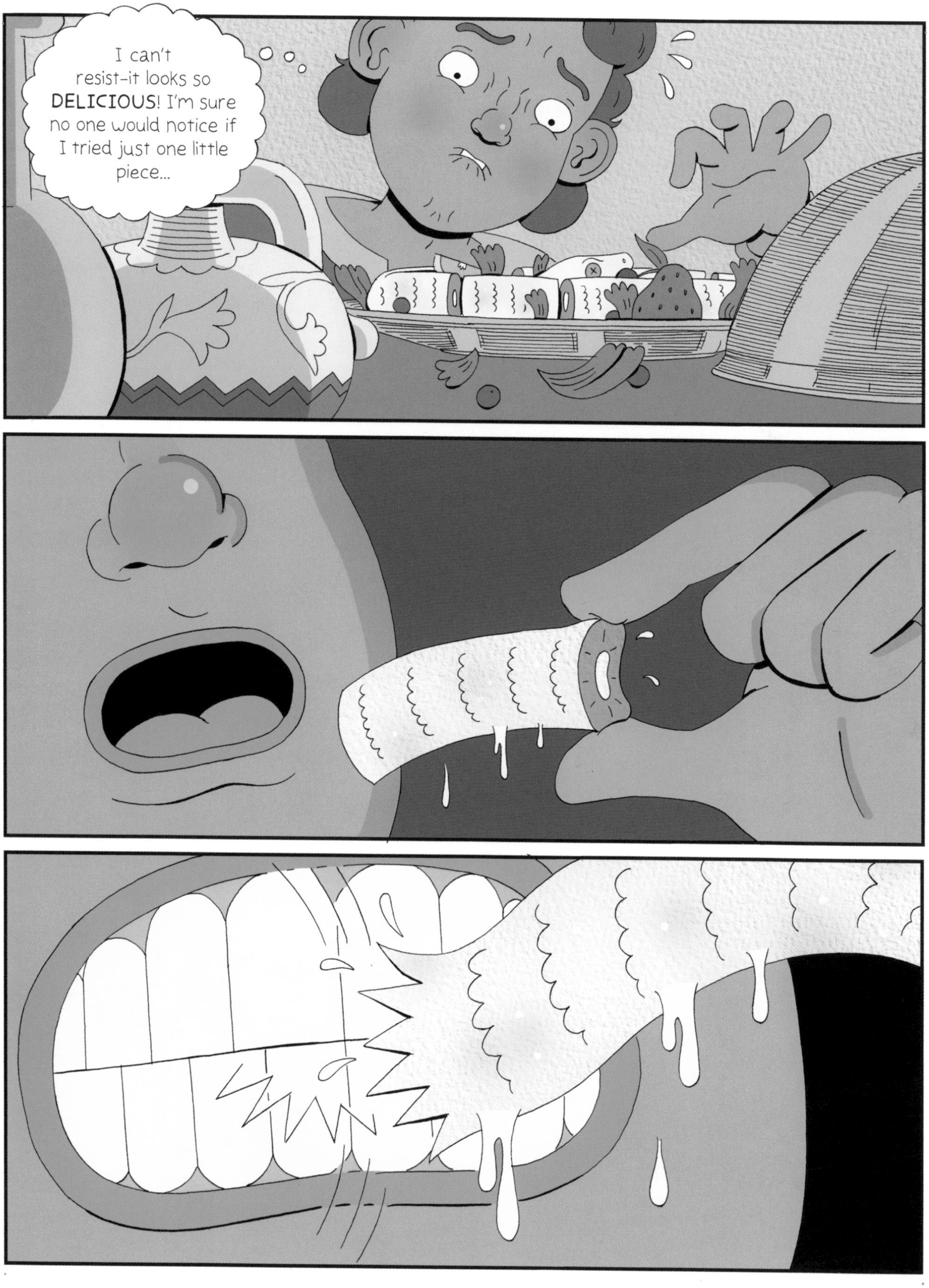
I can't resist–it looks so DELICIOUS! I'm sure no one would notice if I tried just one little piece...

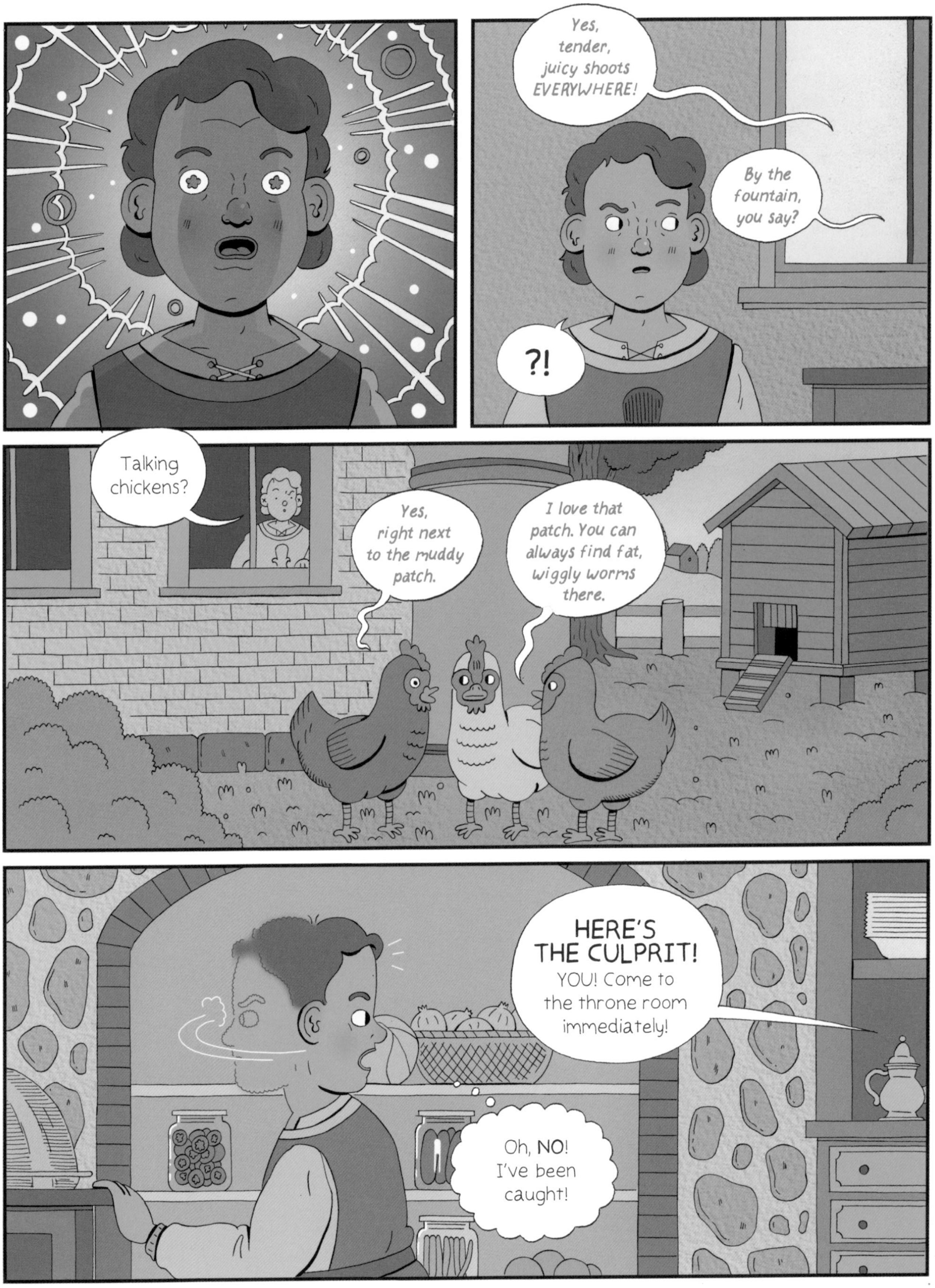
Yes, tender, juicy shoots EVERYWHERE!
By the fountain, you say?
?!
Talking chickens?
Yes, right next to the muddy patch.
I love that patch. You can always find fat, wiggly worms there.
HERE'S THE CULPRIT! YOU! Come to the throne room immediately!
Oh, NO! I've been caught!

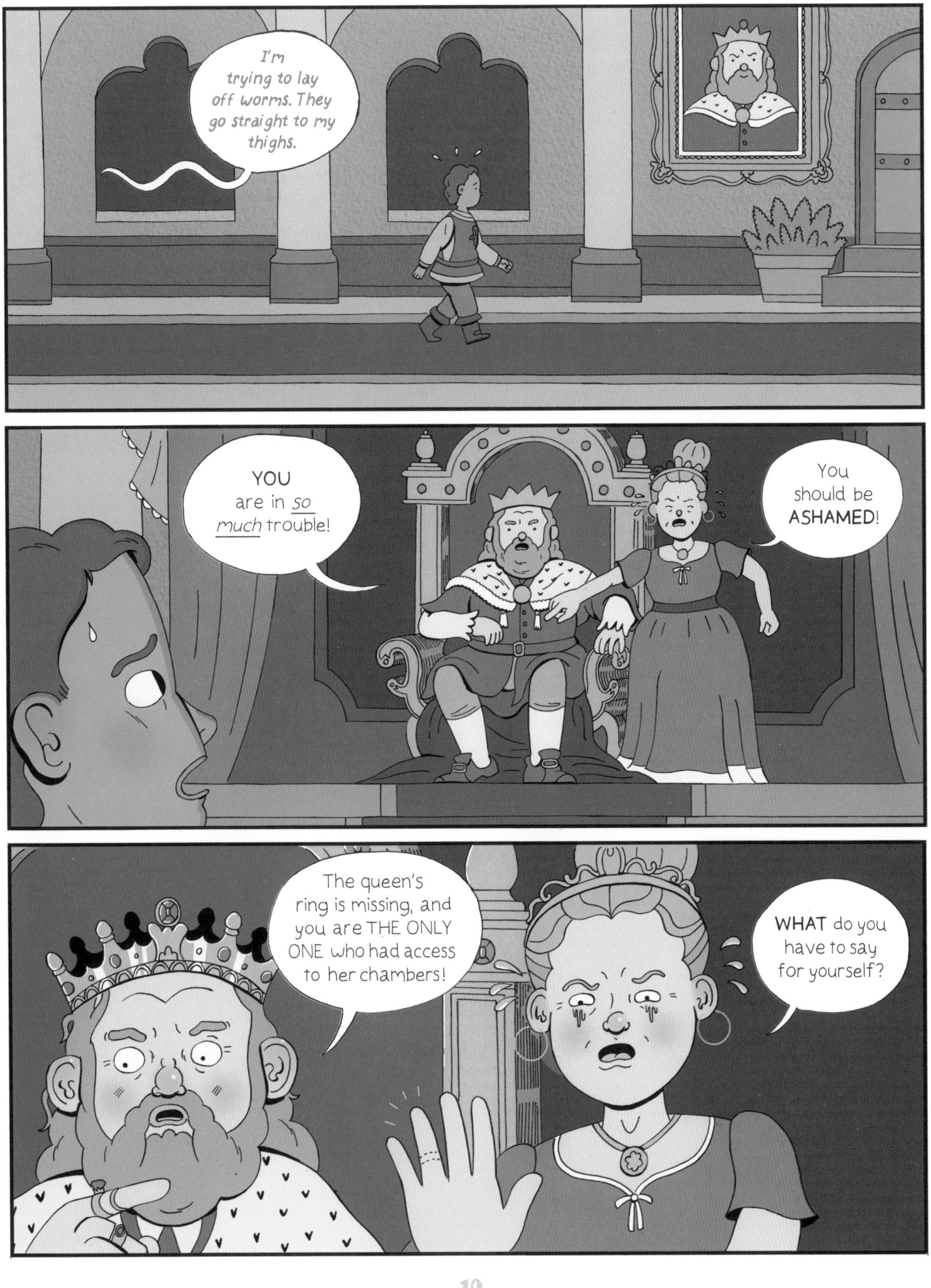
I'm trying to lay off worms. They go straight to my thighs.
YOU are in so much trouble!
You should be ASHAMED!
The queen's ring is missing, and you are THE ONLY ONE who had access to her chambers!
WHAT do you have to say for yourself?

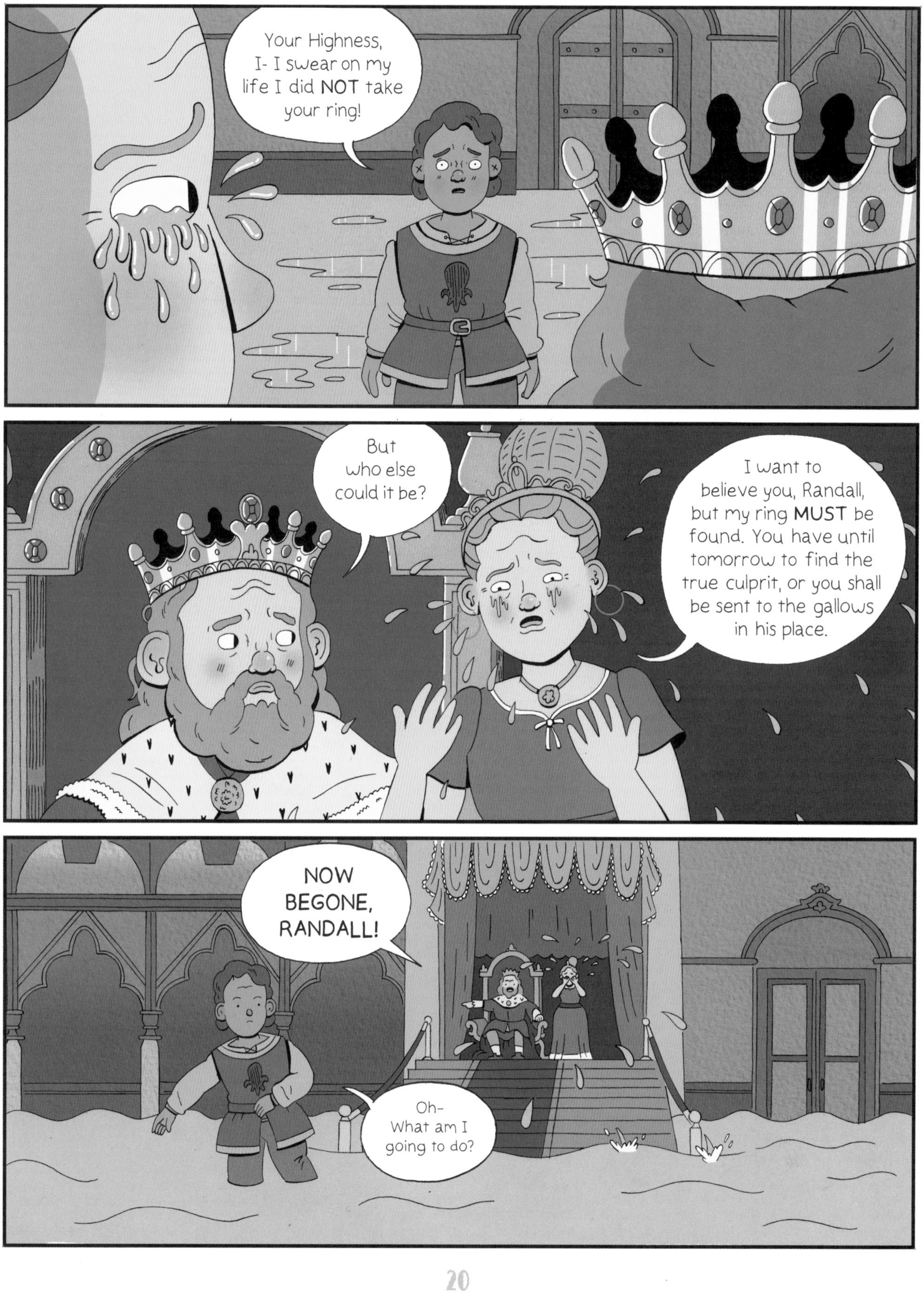
Your Highness, I- I swear on my life I did NOT take your ring!
But who else could it be?
I want to believe you, Randall, but my ring MUST be found. You have until tomorrow to find the true culprit, or you shall be sent to the gallows in his place.
NOW BEGONE, RANDALL!
Oh- What am I going to do?

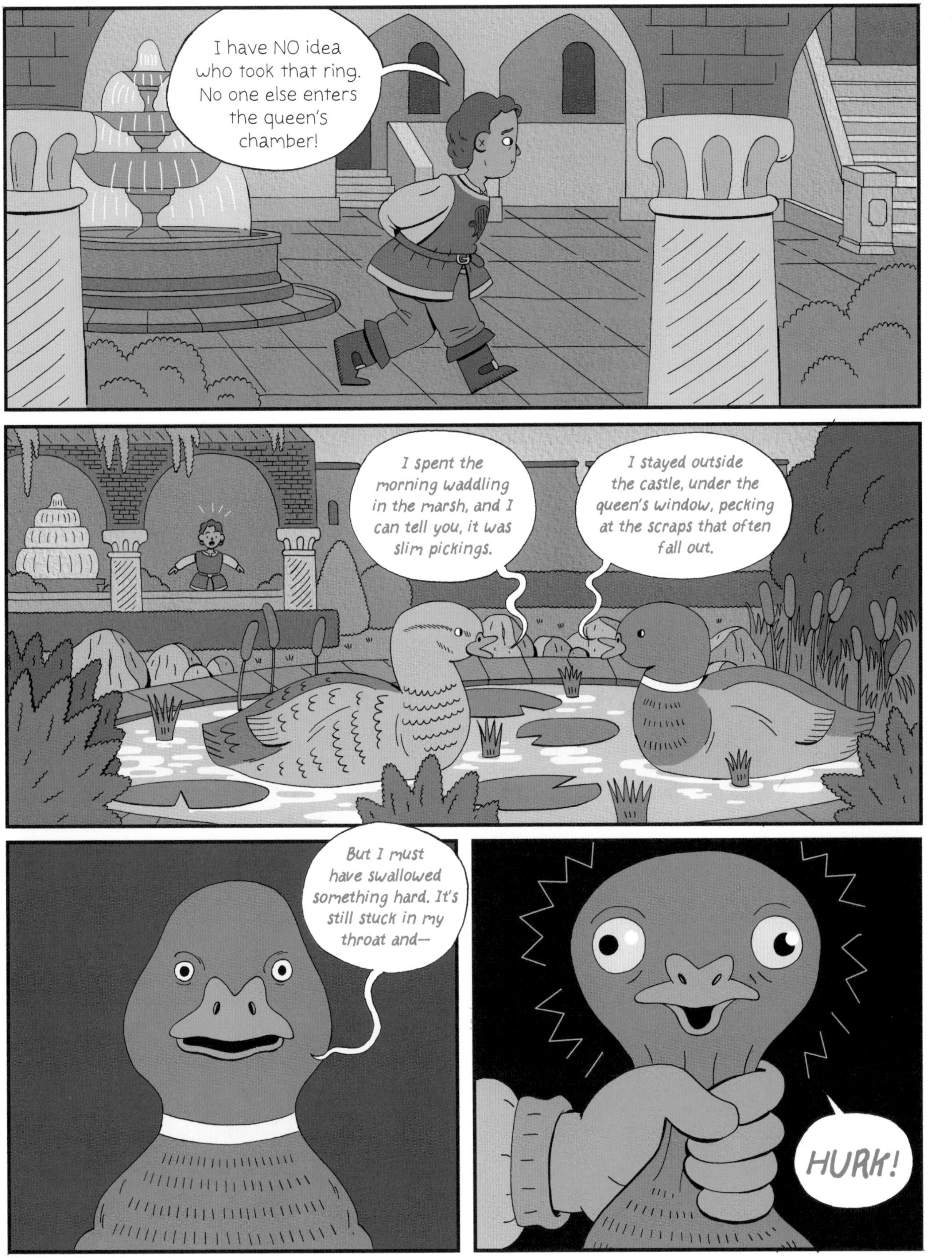
I have NO idea who took that ring. No one else enters the queen's chamber!
I spent the morning waddling in the marsh, and I can tell you, it was slim pickings.
I stayed outside the castle, under the queen's window, pecking at the scraps that often fall out.
But I must have swallowed something hard. It's still stuck in my throat and--
HURK!

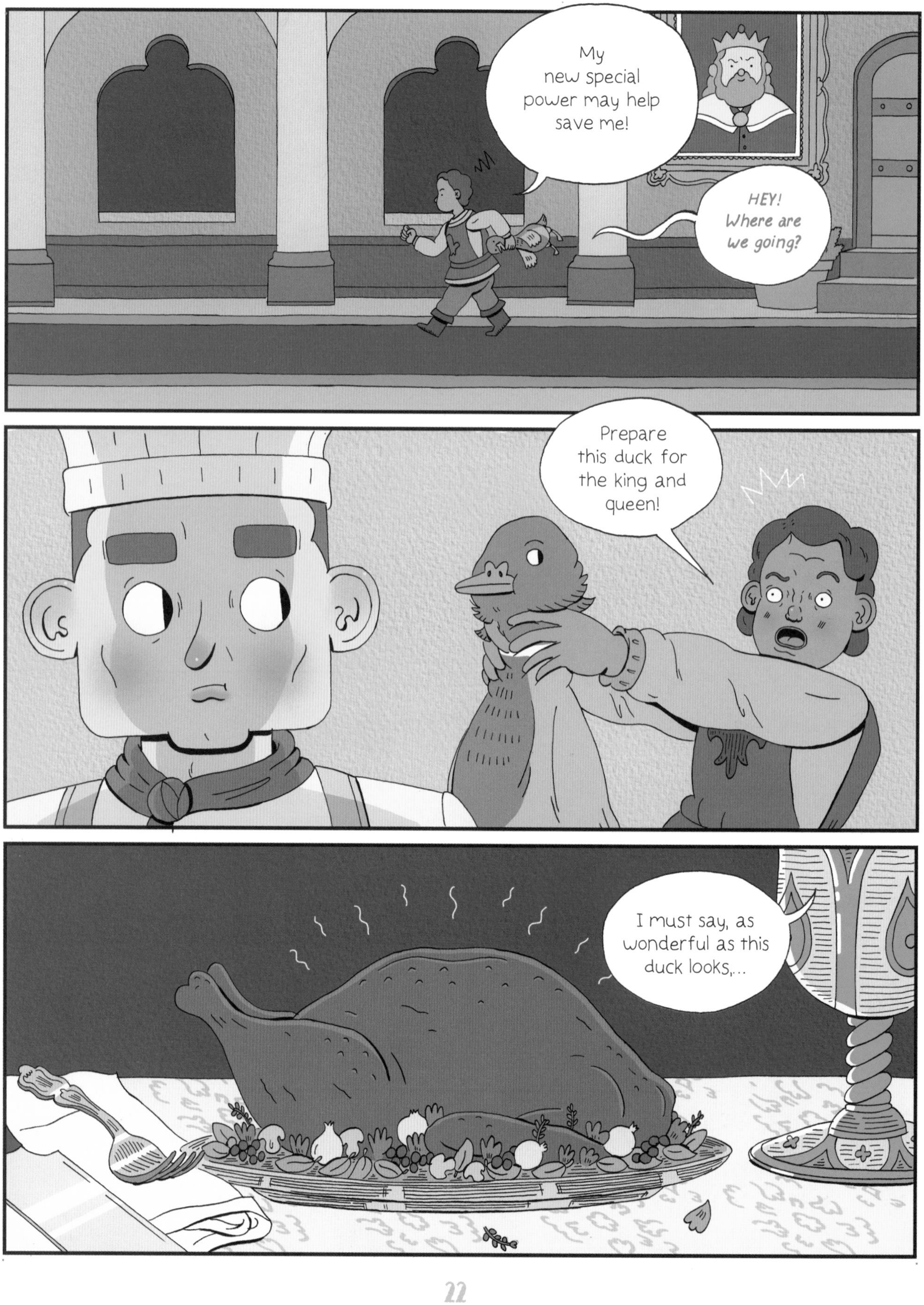
My new special power may help save me!
HEY! Where are we going?
Prepare this duck for the king and queen!
I must say, as wonderful as this duck looks,...

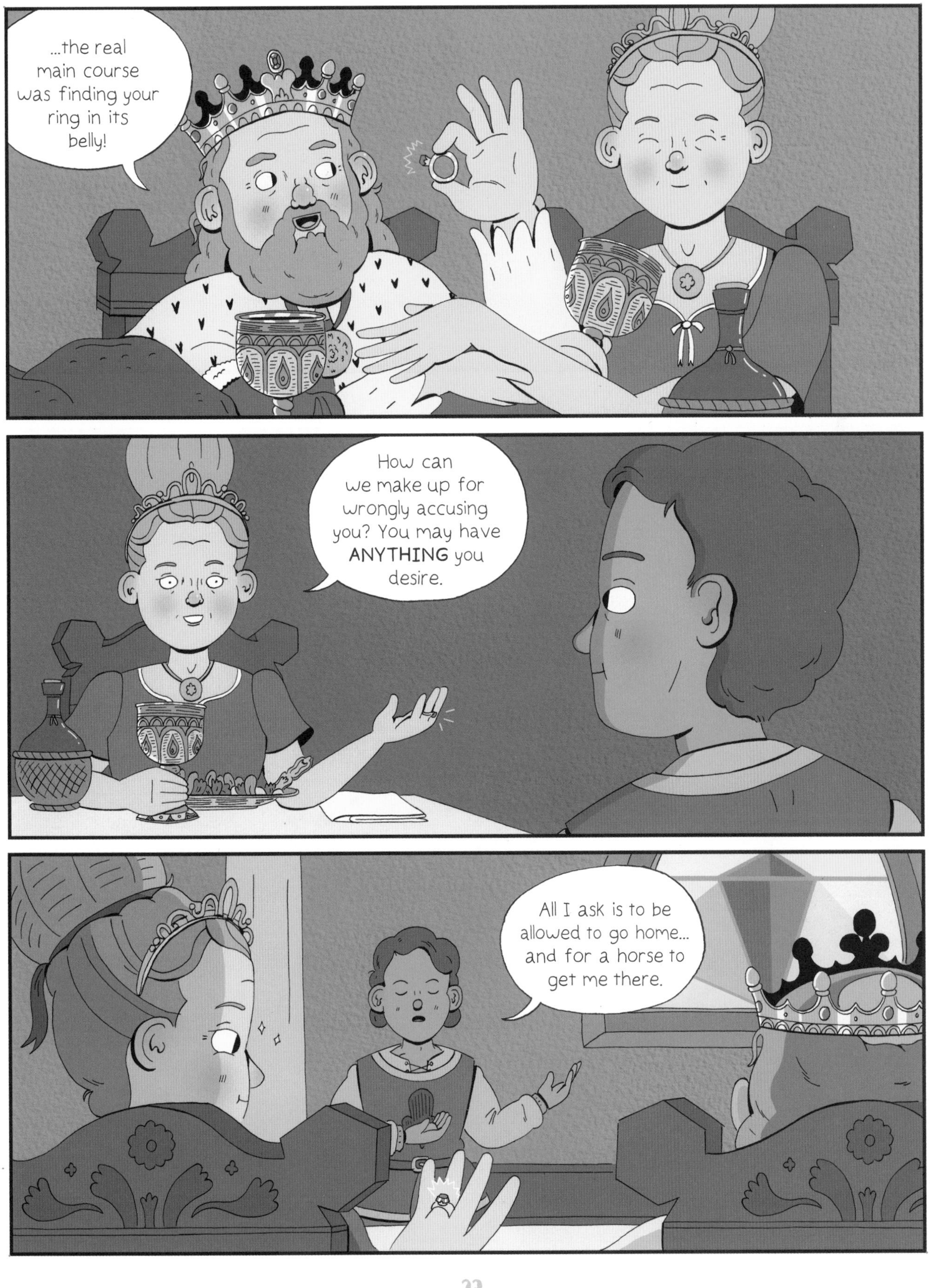
...the real main course was finding your ring in its belly!
How can we make up for wrongly accusing you? You may have **ANYTHING** you desire.
All I ask is to be allowed to go home... and for a horse to get me there.

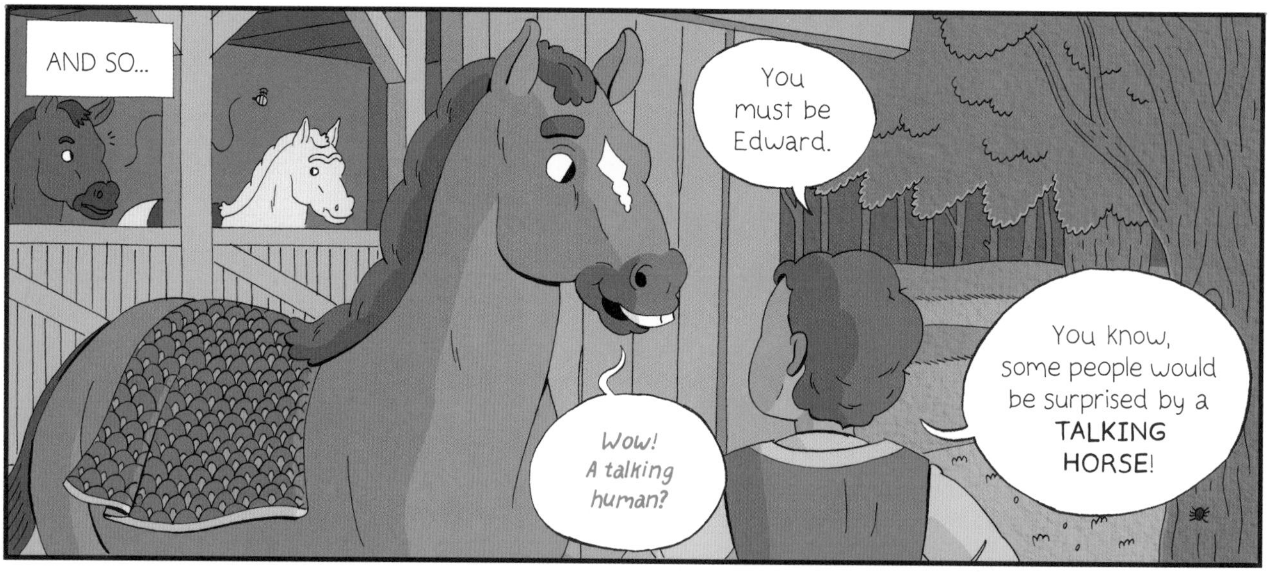
AND SO...
You must be Edward.
Wow! A talking human?
You know, some people would be surprised by a TALKING HORSE!

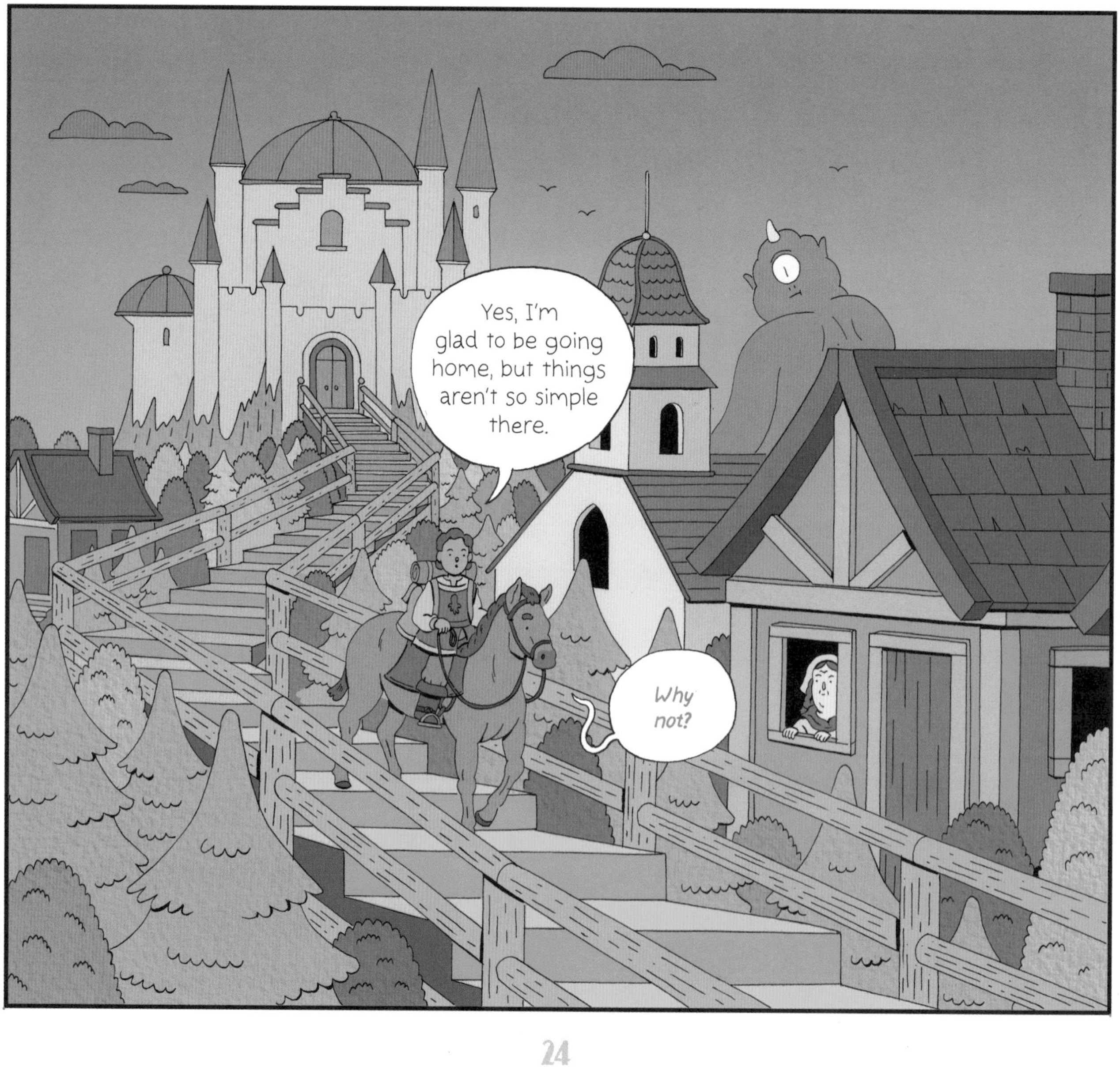
Yes, I'm glad to be going home, but things aren't so simple there.
Why not?

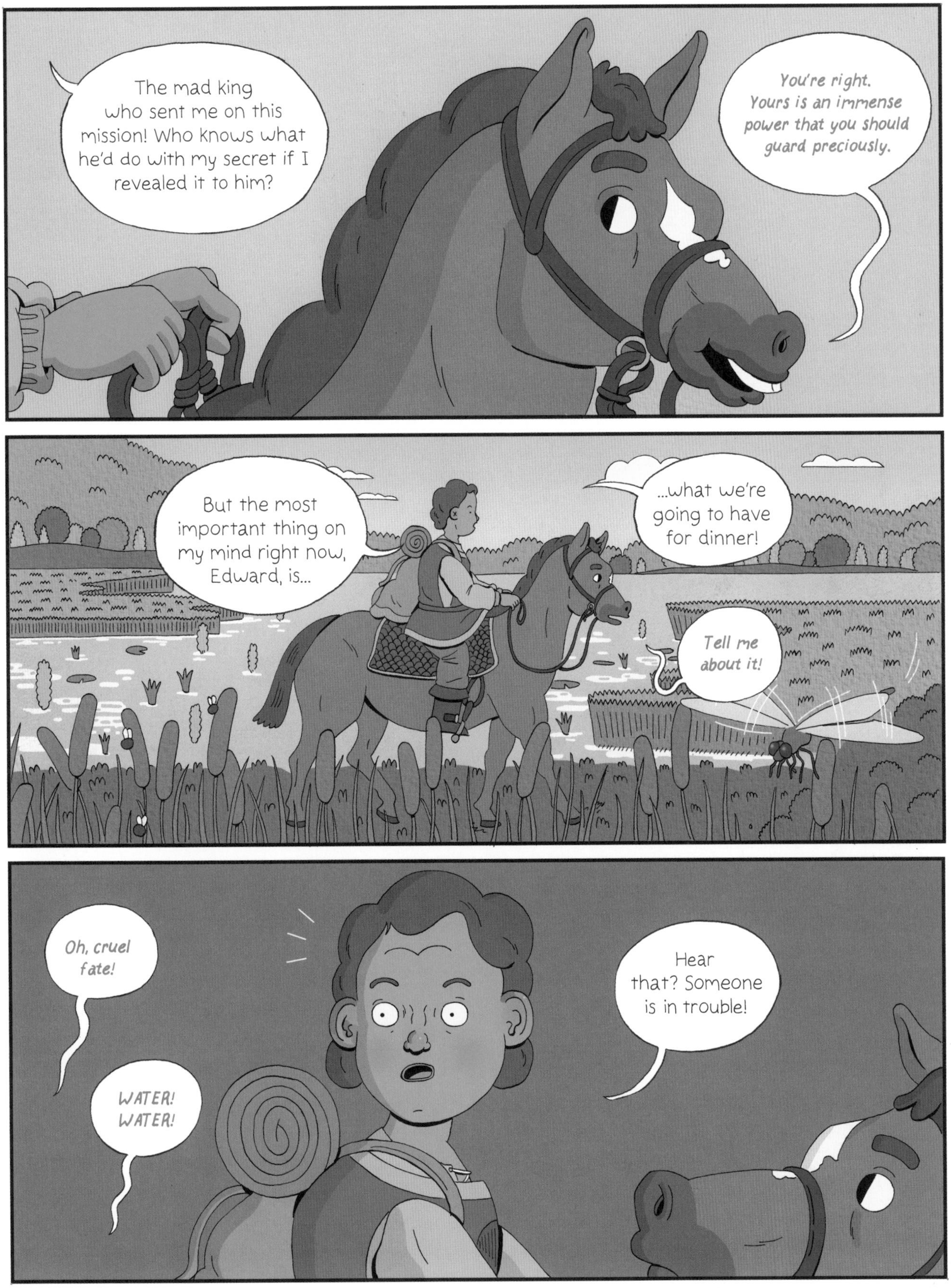
The mad king who sent me on this mission! Who knows what he'd do with my secret if I revealed it to him?
You're right. Yours is an immense power that you should guard preciously.
But the most important thing on my mind right now, Edward, is...
...what we're going to have for dinner!
Tell me about it!
Oh, cruel fate!
WATER! WATER!
Hear that? Someone is in trouble!

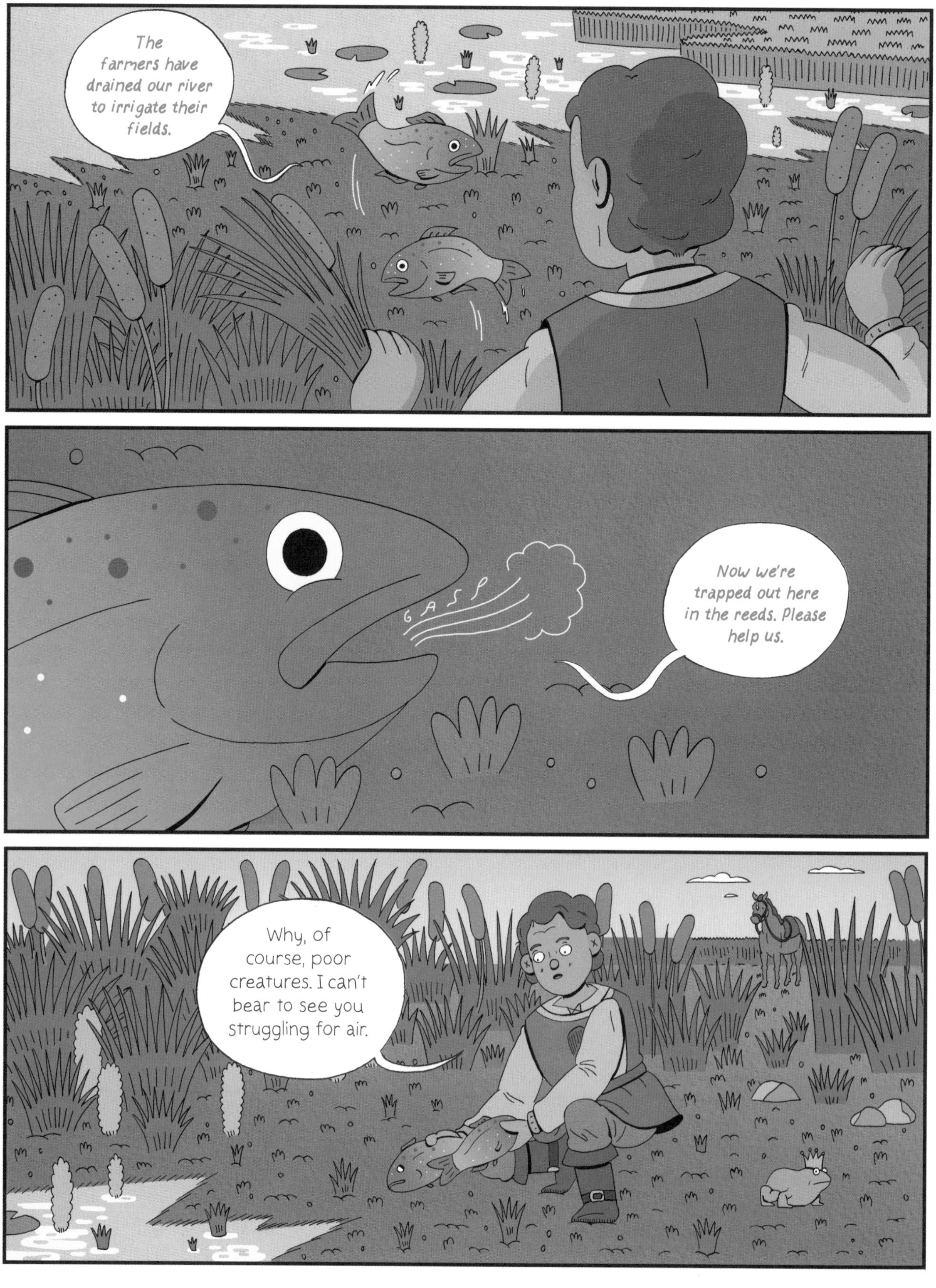
The farmers have drained our river to irrigate their fields.
GASP
Now we're trapped out here in the reeds. Please help us.
Why, of course, poor creatures. I can't bear to see you struggling for air.

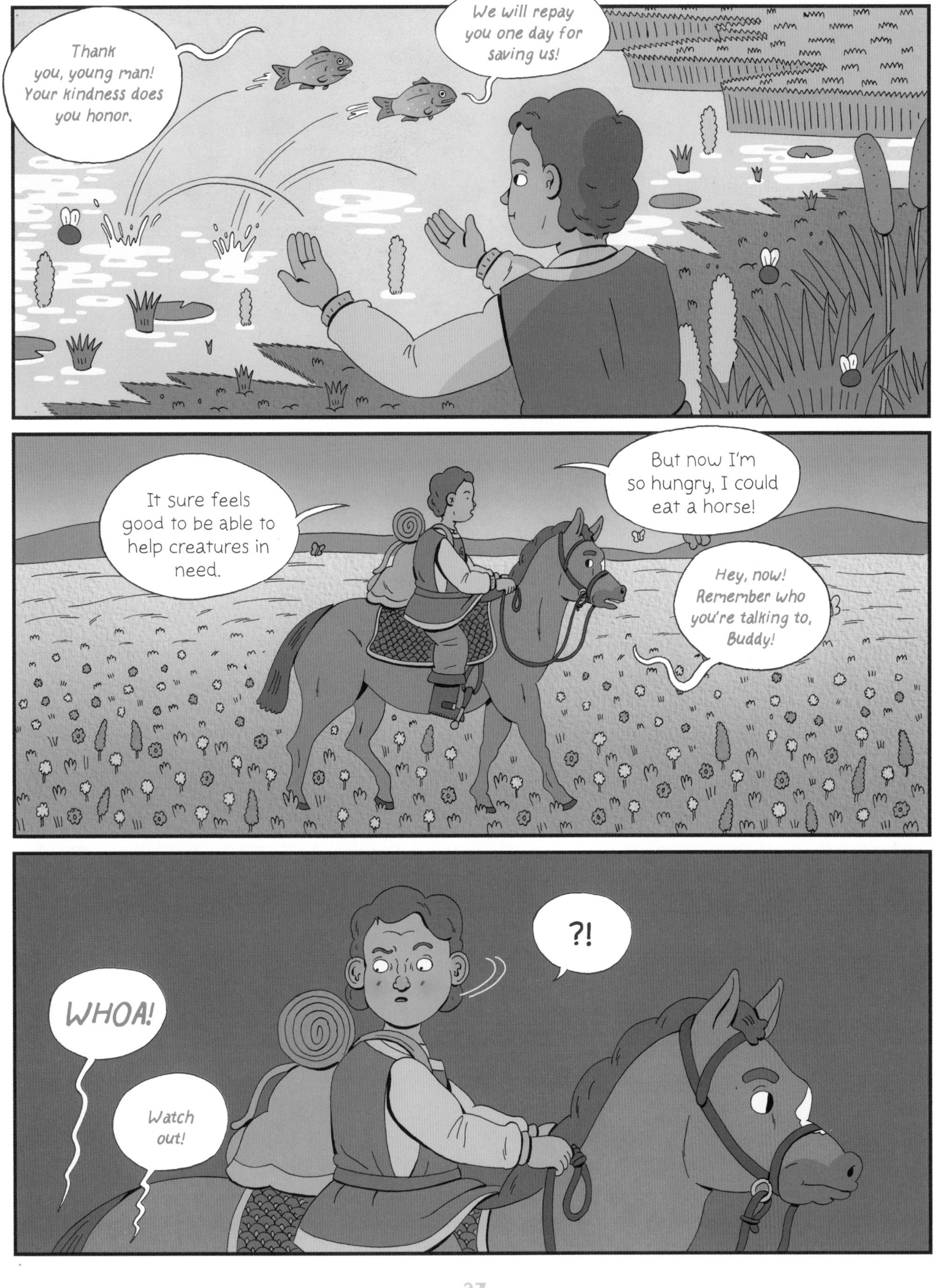
Thank you, young man! Your kindness does you honor.
We will repay you one day for saving us!
It sure feels good to be able to help creatures in need.
But now I'm so hungry, I could eat a horse!
Hey, now! Remember who you're talking to, Buddy!
WHOA!
Watch out!
?!

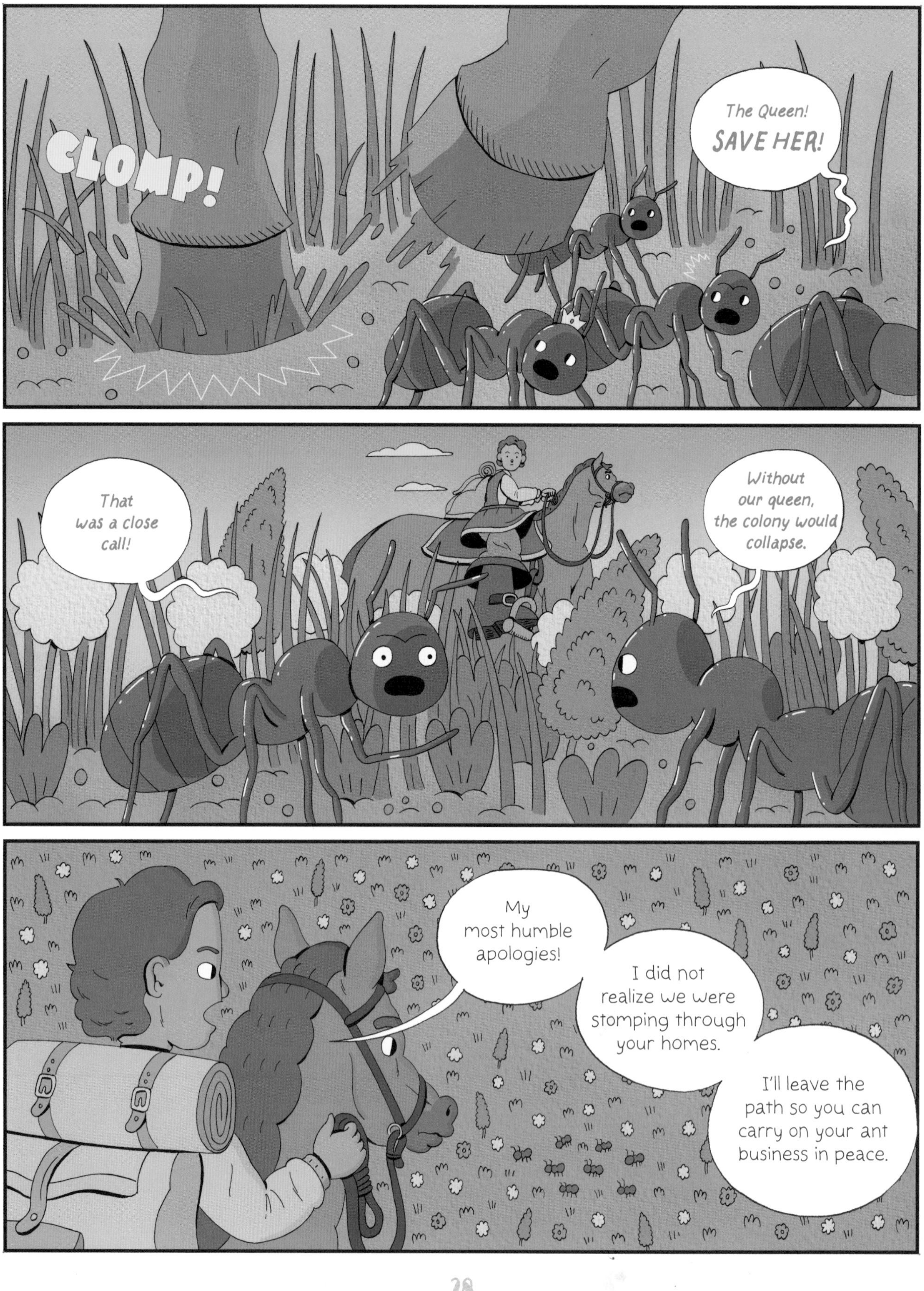
CLOMP!
The Queen!
SAVE HER!
That was a close call!
Without our queen, the colony would collapse.
My most humble apologies!
I did not realize we were stomping through your homes.
I'll leave the path so you can carry on your ant business in peace.

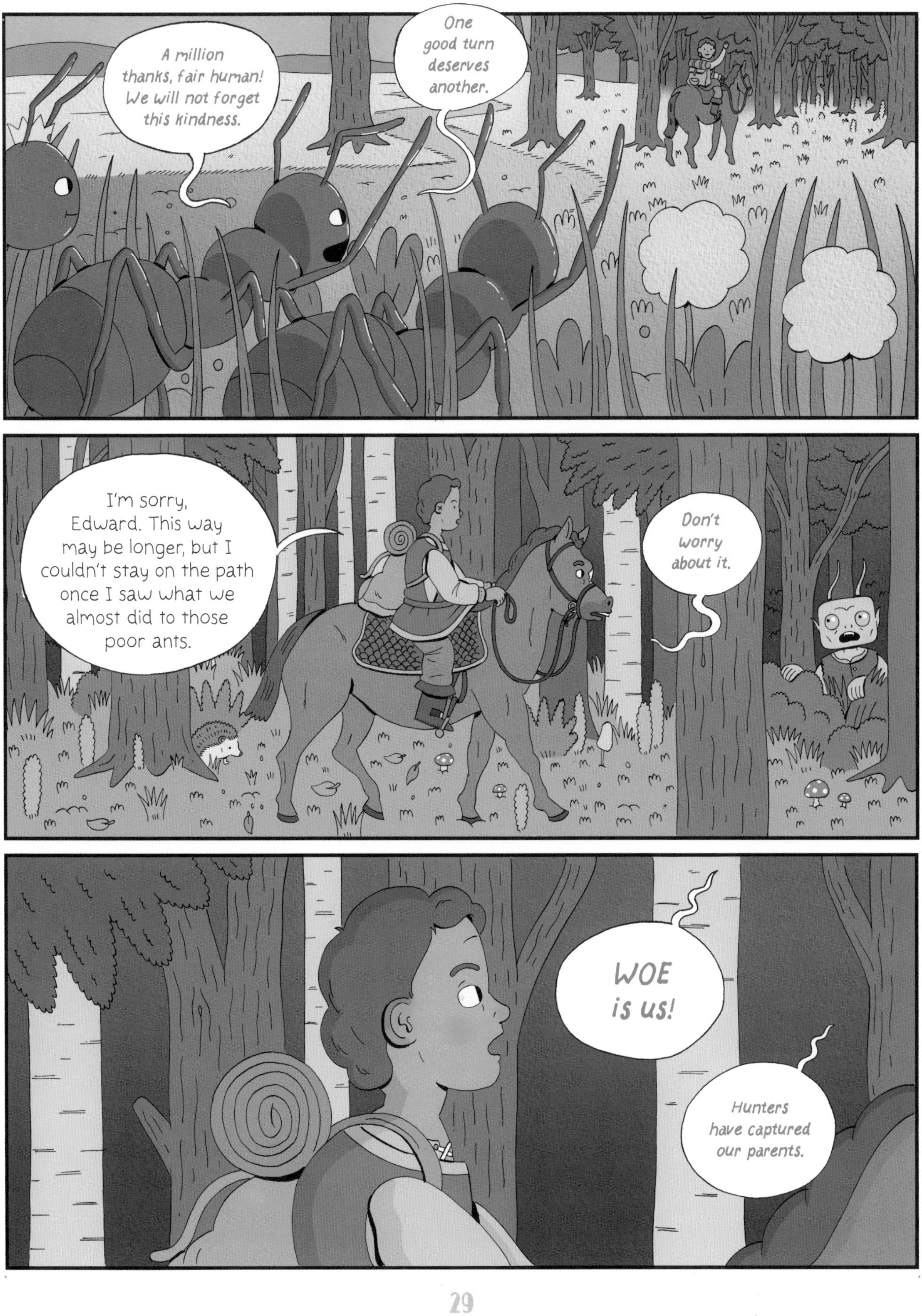
A million thanks, fair human! We will not forget this kindness.
One good turn deserves another.
I'm sorry, Edward. This way may be longer, but I couldn't stay on the path once I saw what we almost did to those poor ants.
Don't worry about it.
WOE is us!
Hunters have captured our parents.

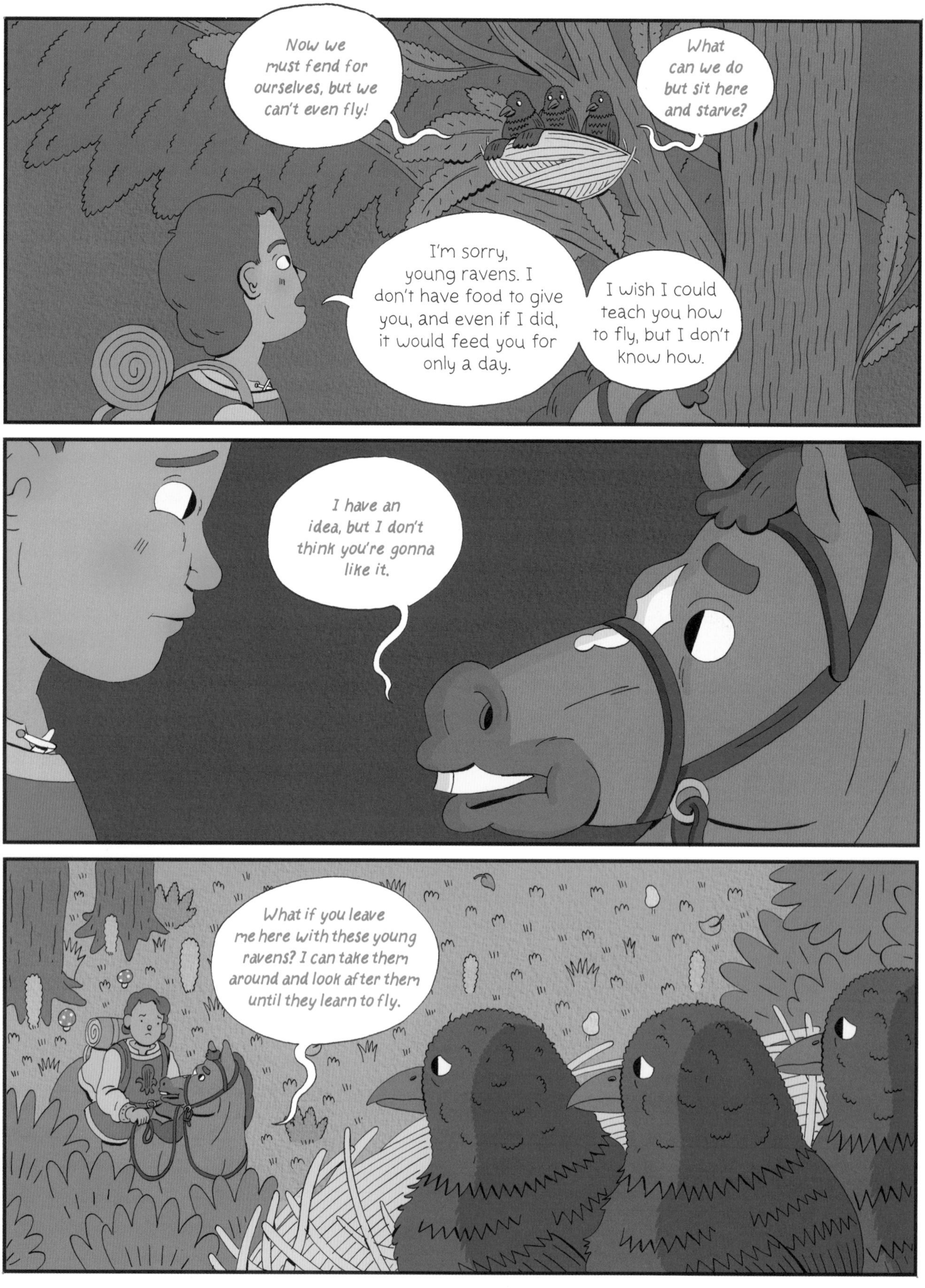

Now we must fend for ourselves, but we can't even fly!
What can we do but sit here and starve?
I'm sorry, young ravens. I don't have food to give you, and even if I did, it would feed you for only a day.
I wish I could teach you how to fly, but I don't know how.
I have an idea, but I don't think you're gonna like it.
What if you leave me here with these young ravens? I can take them around and look after them until they learn to fly.

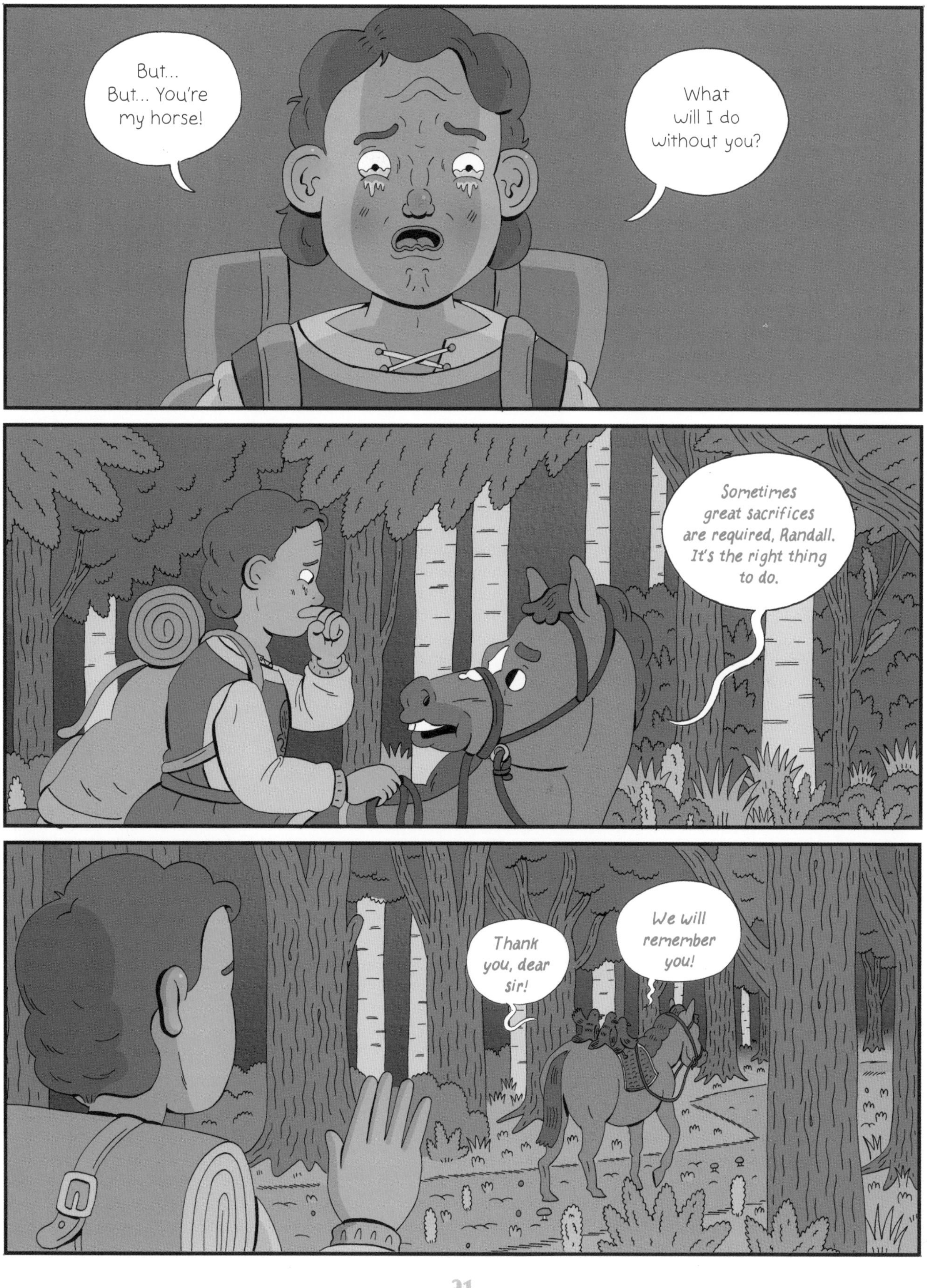
But... But... You're my horse!
What will I do without you?
Sometimes great sacrifices are required, Randall. It's the right thing to do.
Thank you, dear sir!
We will remember you!

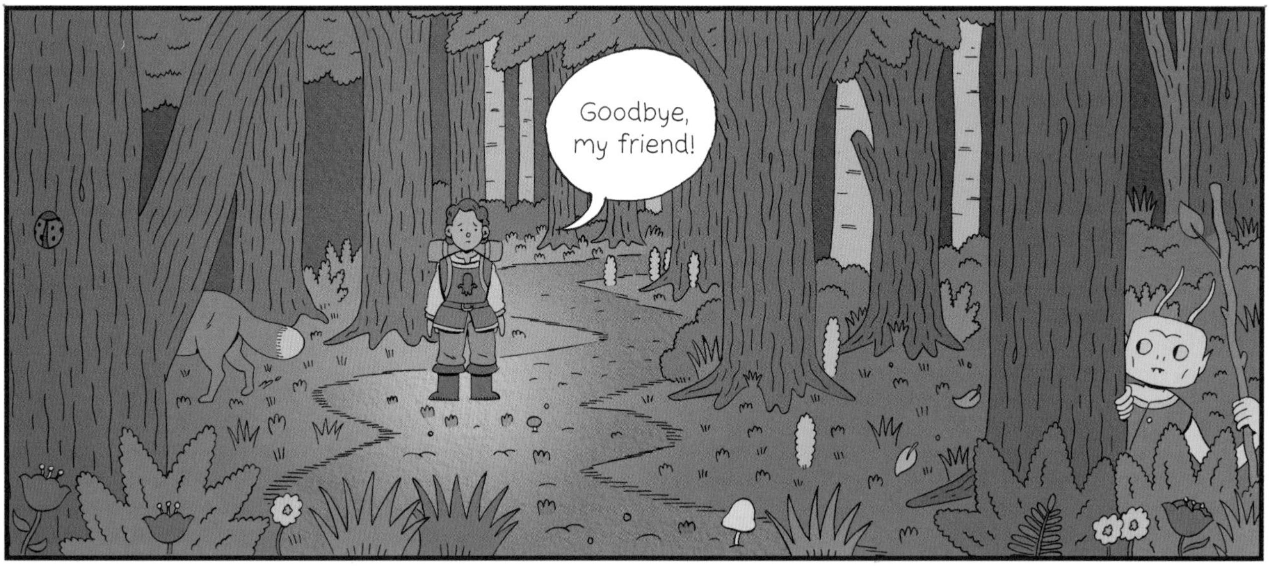
Goodbye, my friend!

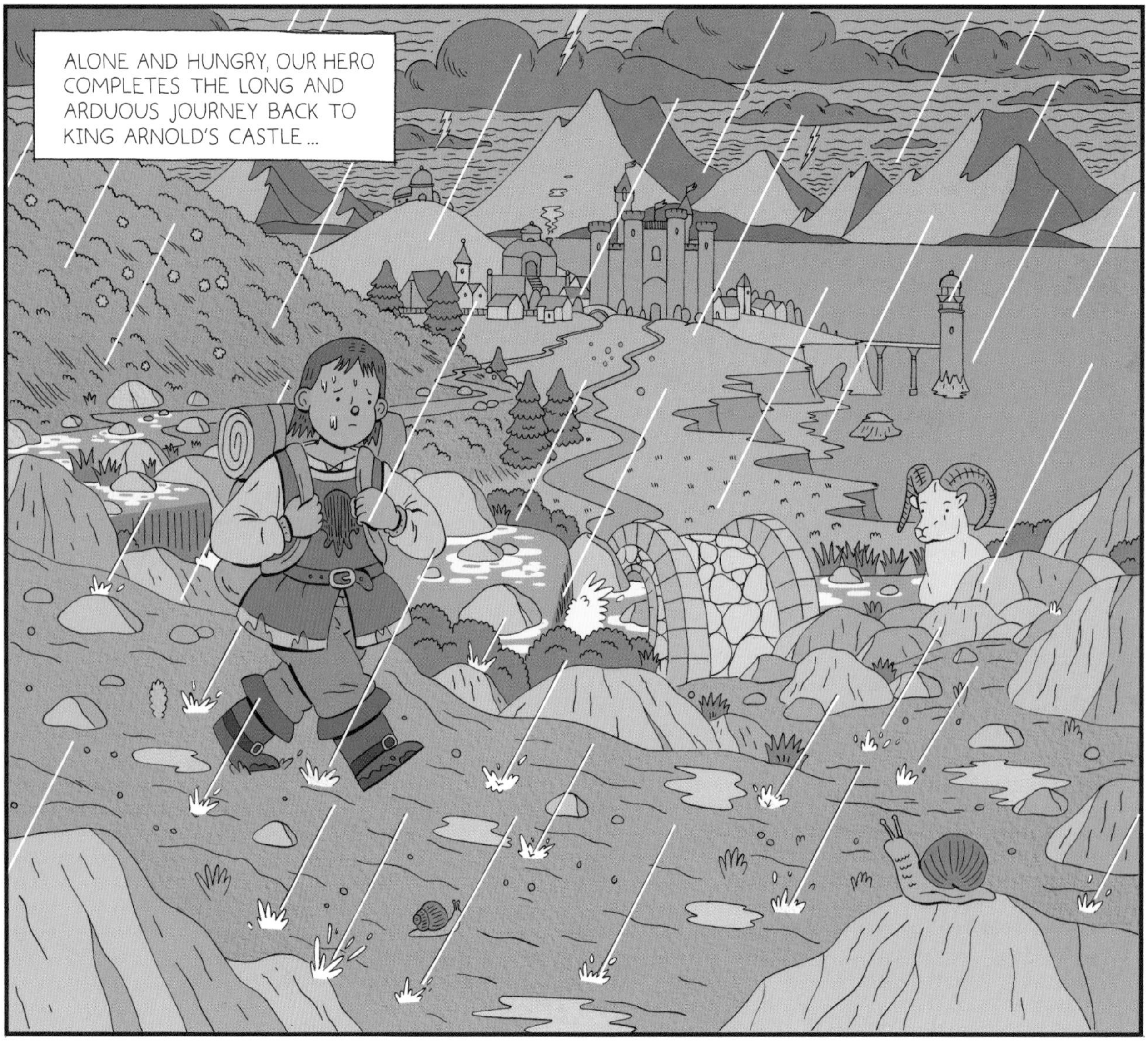
ALONE AND HUNGRY, OUR HERO COMPLETES THE LONG AND ARDUOUS JOURNEY BACK TO KING ARNOLD'S CASTLE...

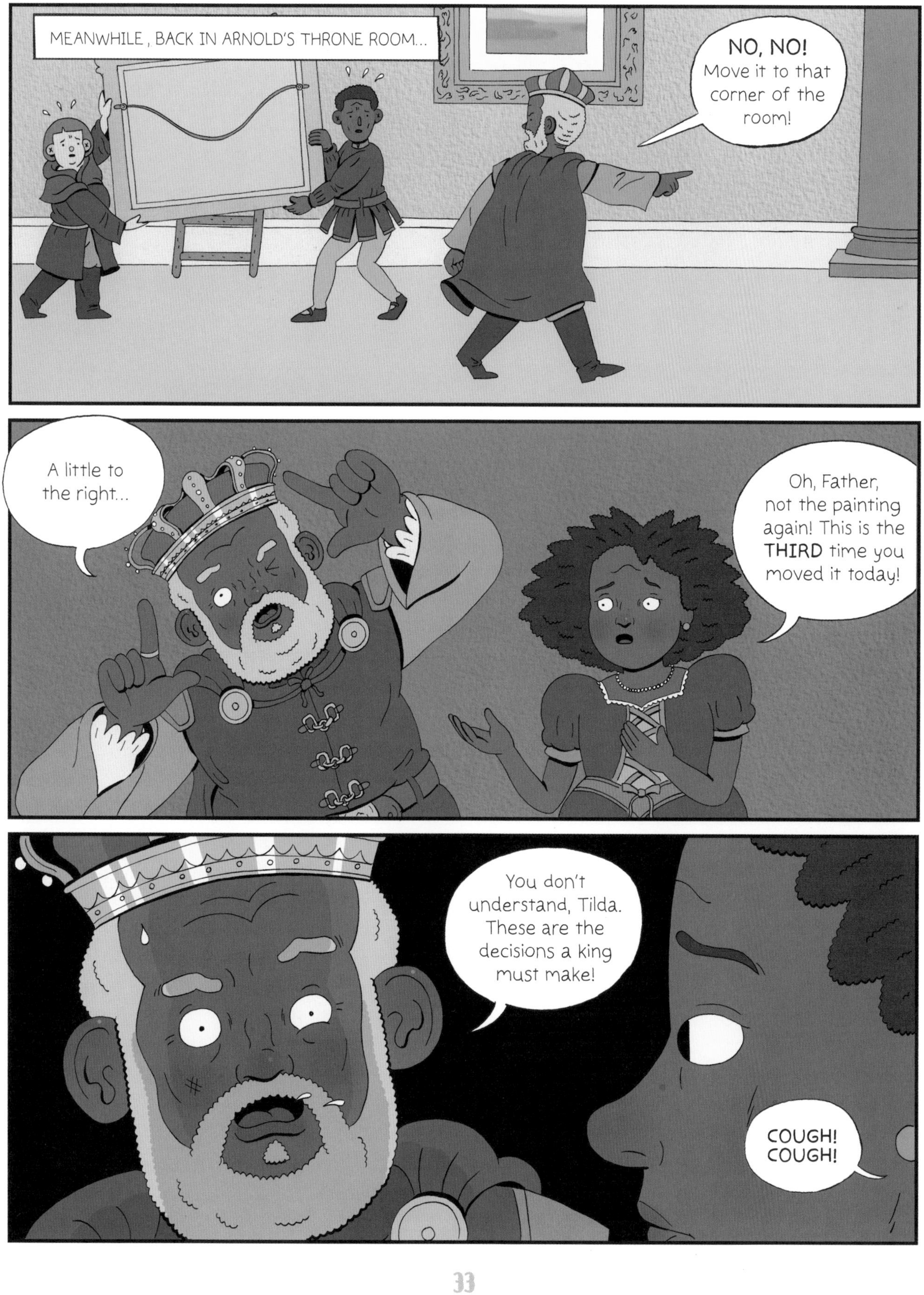
MEANWHILE, BACK IN ARNOLD'S THRONE ROOM...
NO, NO! Move it to that corner of the room!
A little to the right...
Oh, Father, not the painting again! This is the THIRD time you moved it today!
You don't understand, Tilda. These are the decisions a king must make!
COUGH! COUGH!

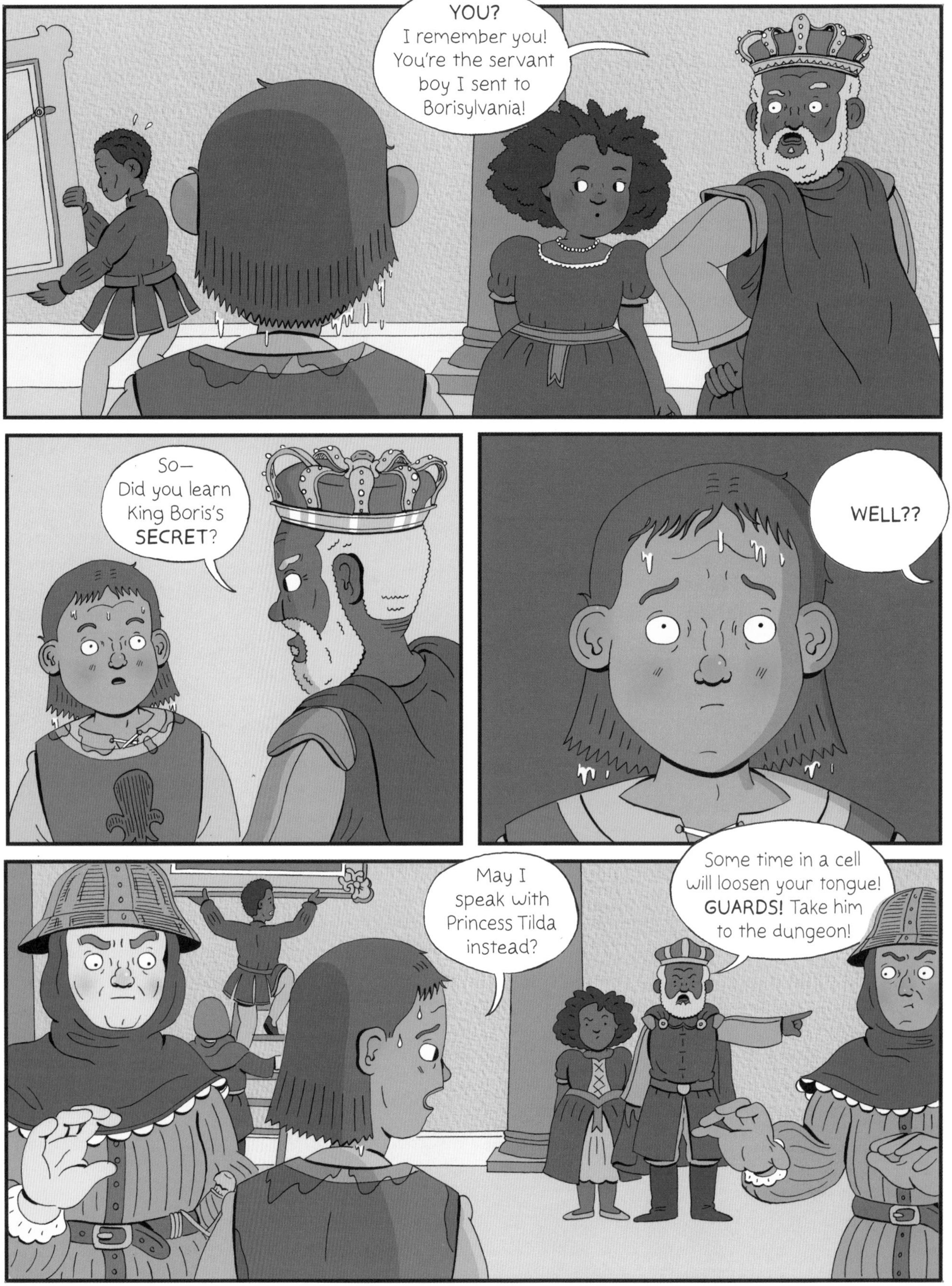
YOU?
I remember you! You're the servant boy I sent to Borisylvania!
So— Did you learn King Boris's SECRET?
WELL??
May I speak with Princess Tilda instead?
Some time in a cell will loosen your tongue! GUARDS! Take him to the dungeon!

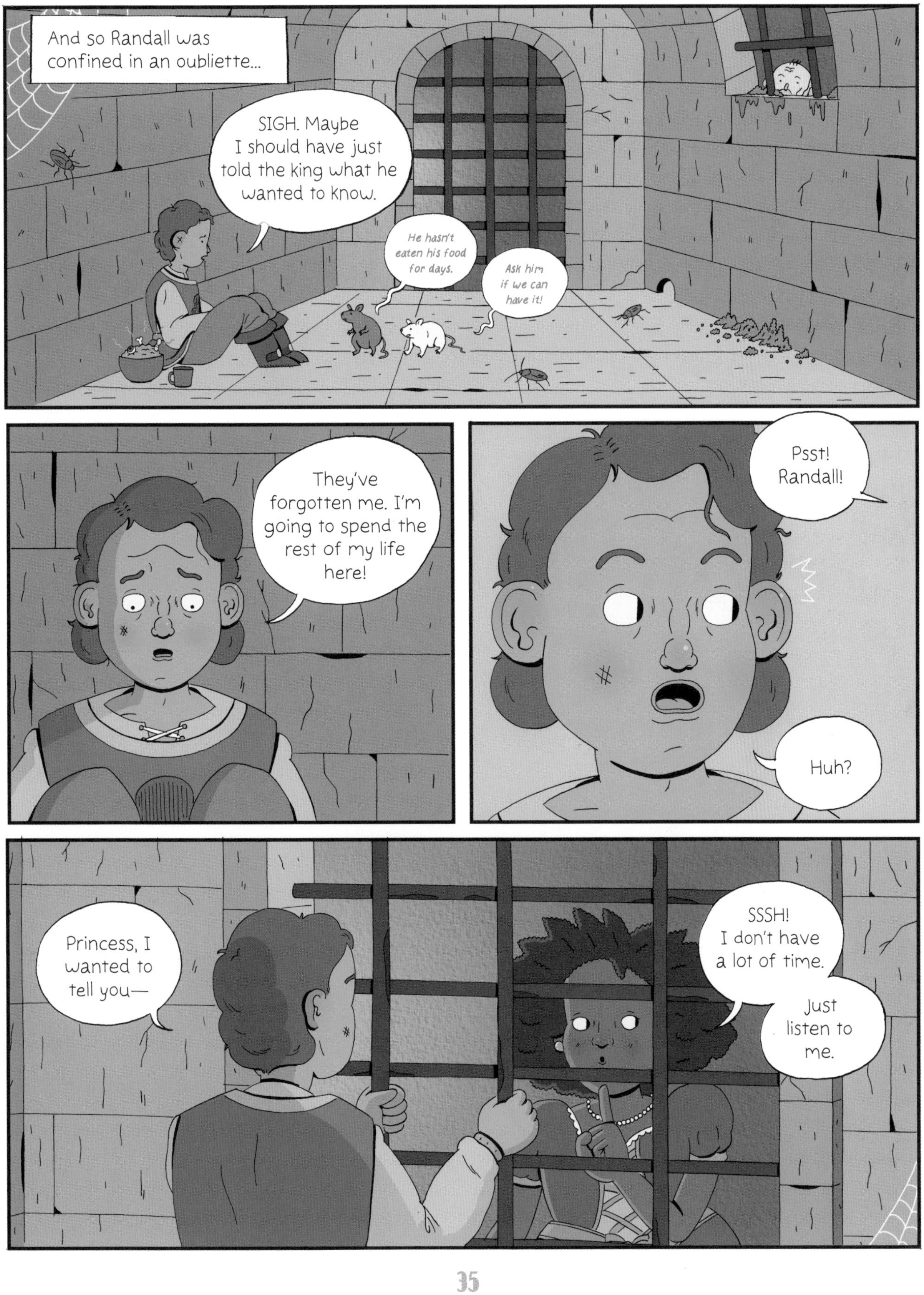
And so Randall was confined in an oubliette...
SIGH. Maybe I should have just told the king what he wanted to know.
He hasn't eaten his food for days.
Ask him if we can have it!
They've forgotten me. I'm going to spend the rest of my life here!
Psst! Randall!
Huh?
Princess, I wanted to tell you—
SSSH! I don't have a lot of time.
Just listen to me.

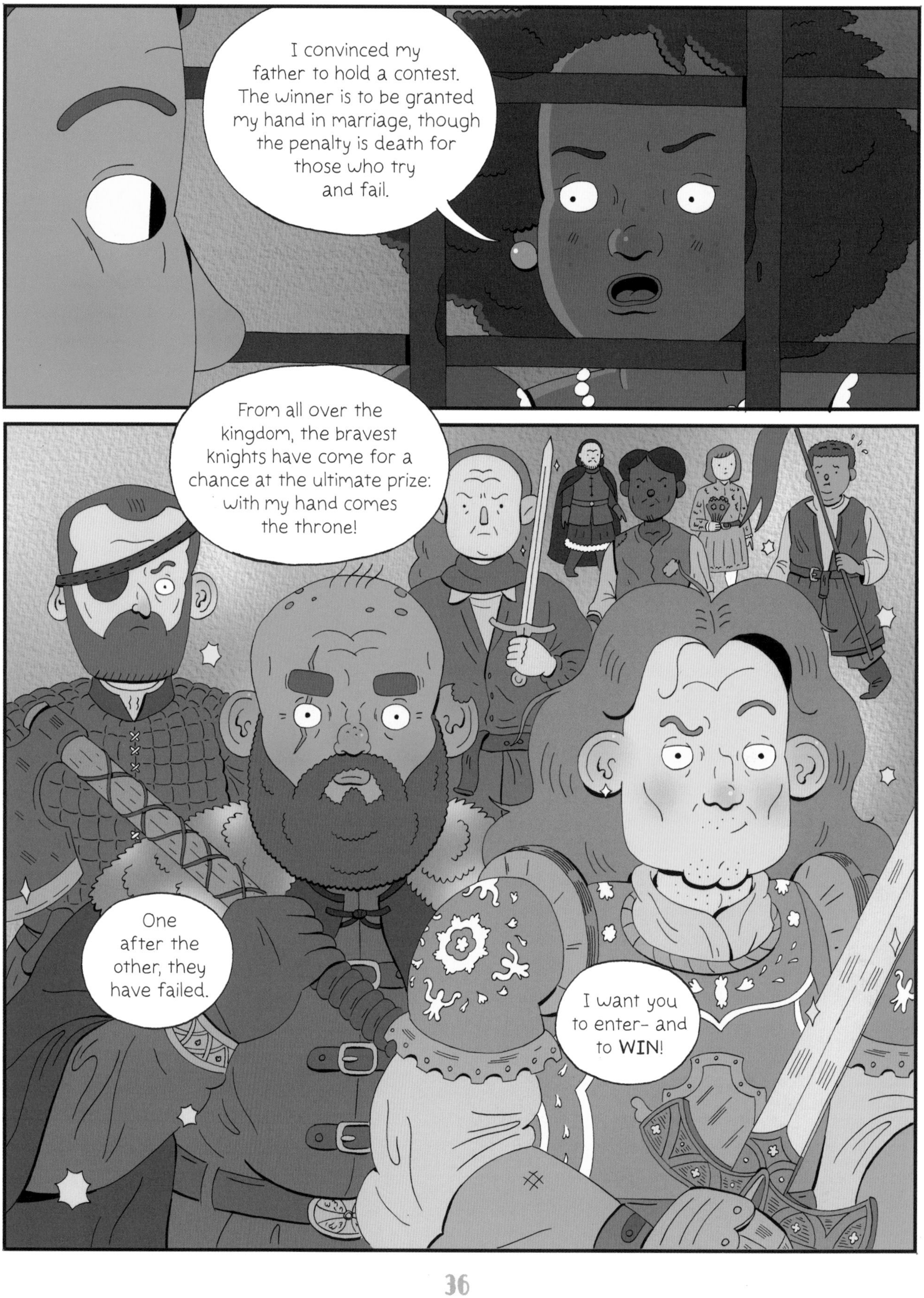
I convinced my father to hold a contest. The winner is to be granted my hand in marriage, though the penalty is death for those who try and fail.
From all over the kingdom, the bravest knights have come for a chance at the ultimate prize: with my hand comes the throne!
One after the other, they have failed.
I want you to enter- and to **WIN**!

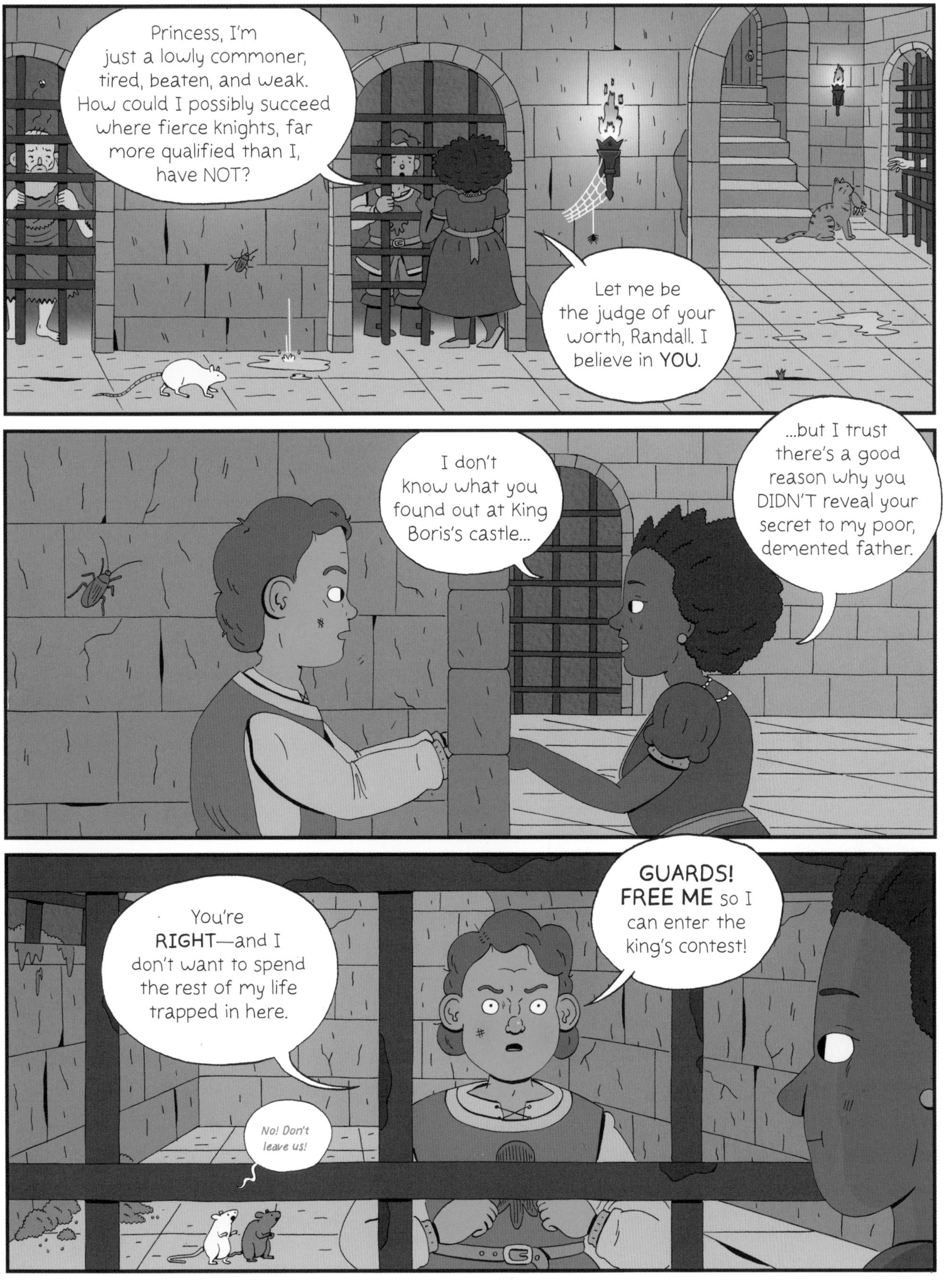
Princess, I'm just a lowly commoner, tired, beaten, and weak. How could I possibly succeed where fierce knights, far more qualified than I, have NOT?
Let me be the judge of your worth, Randall. I believe in **YOU**.
I don't know what you found out at King Boris's castle...
...but I trust there's a good reason why you DIDN'T reveal your secret to my poor, demented father.
You're **RIGHT**—and I don't want to spend the rest of my life trapped in here.
*No! Don't leave us!*
**GUARDS! FREE ME** so I can enter the king's contest!

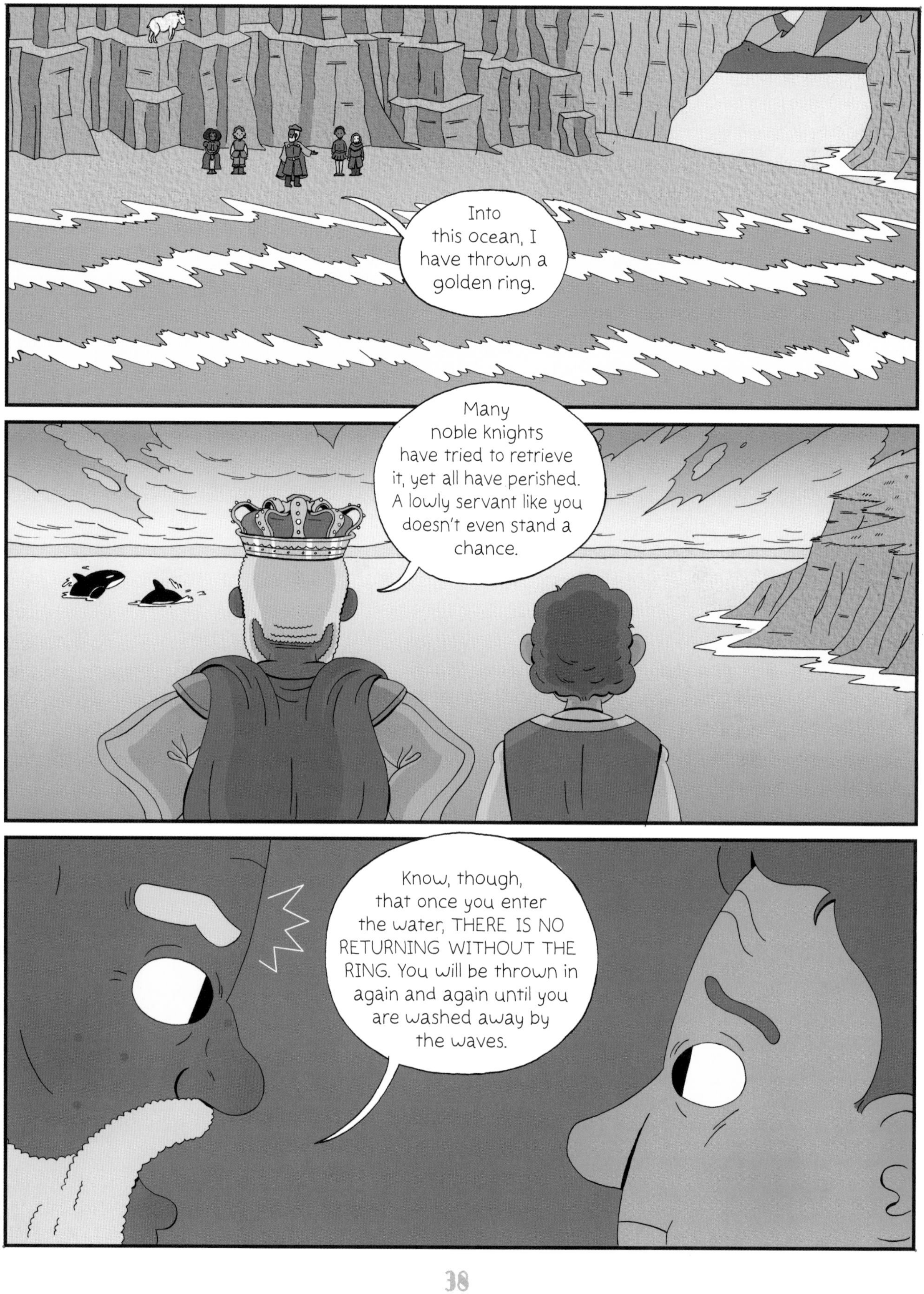
Into this ocean, I have thrown a golden ring.
Many noble knights have tried to retrieve it, yet all have perished. A lowly servant like you doesn't even stand a chance.
Know, though, that once you enter the water, THERE IS NO RETURNING WITHOUT THE RING. You will be thrown in again and again until you are washed away by the waves.

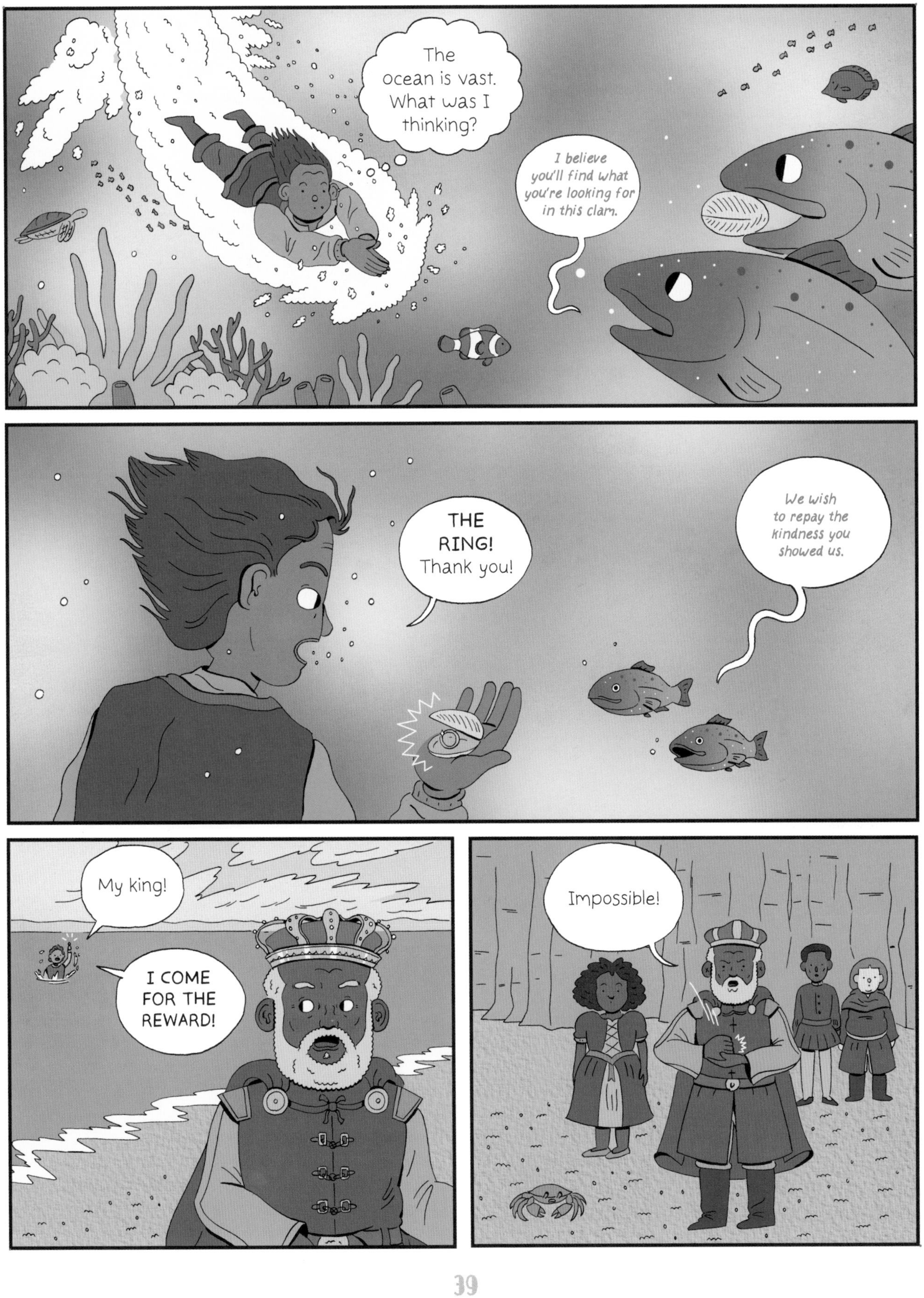
The ocean is vast. What was I thinking?
I believe you'll find what you're looking for in this clam.
THE RING! Thank you!
We wish to repay the kindness you showed us.
My king!
I COME FOR THE REWARD!
Impossible!

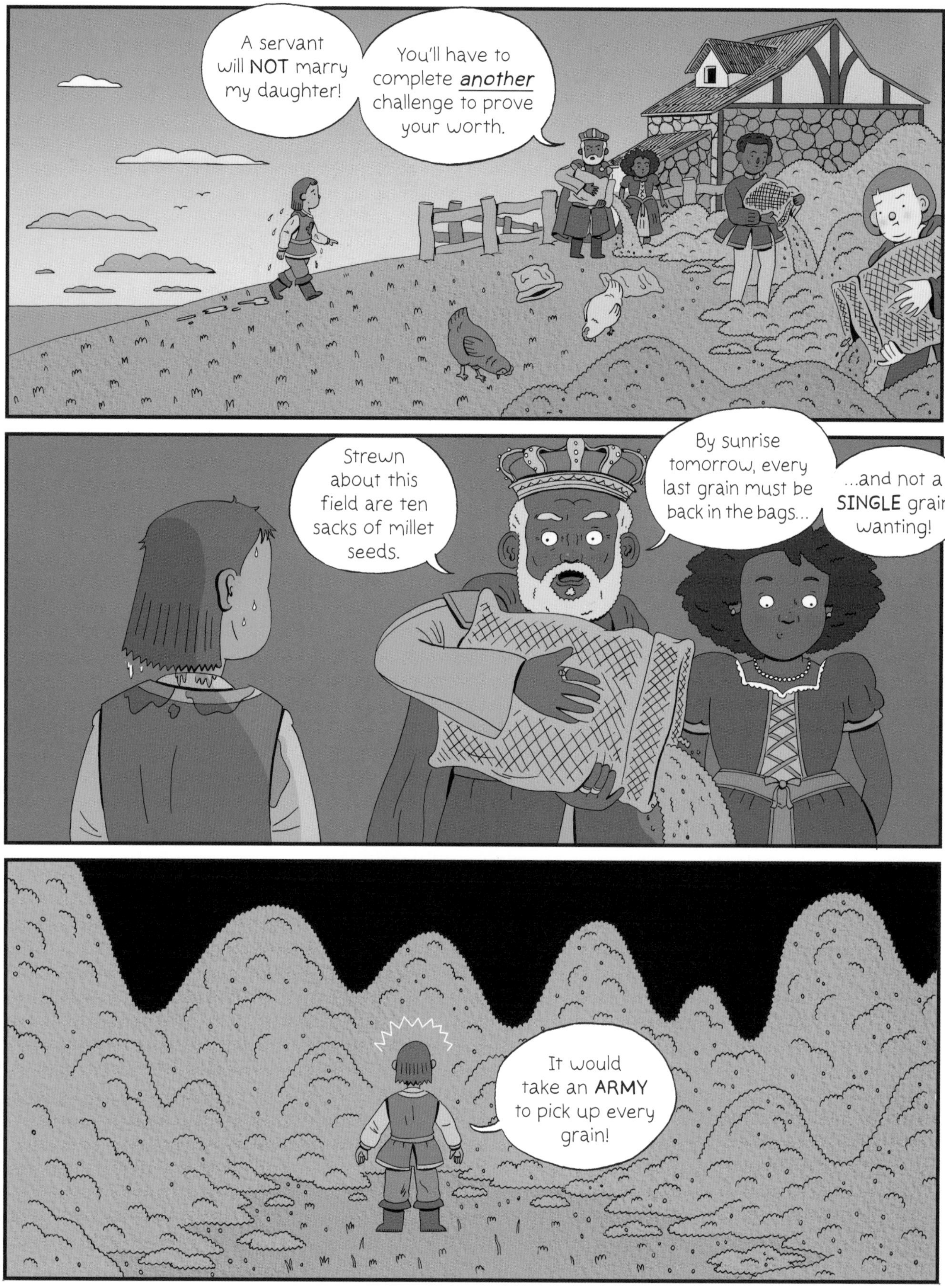
A servant will NOT marry my daughter!
You'll have to complete another challenge to prove your worth.
Strewn about this field are ten sacks of millet seeds.
By sunrise tomorrow, every last grain must be back in the bags...
...and not a SINGLE grain wanting!
It would take an ARMY to pick up every grain!

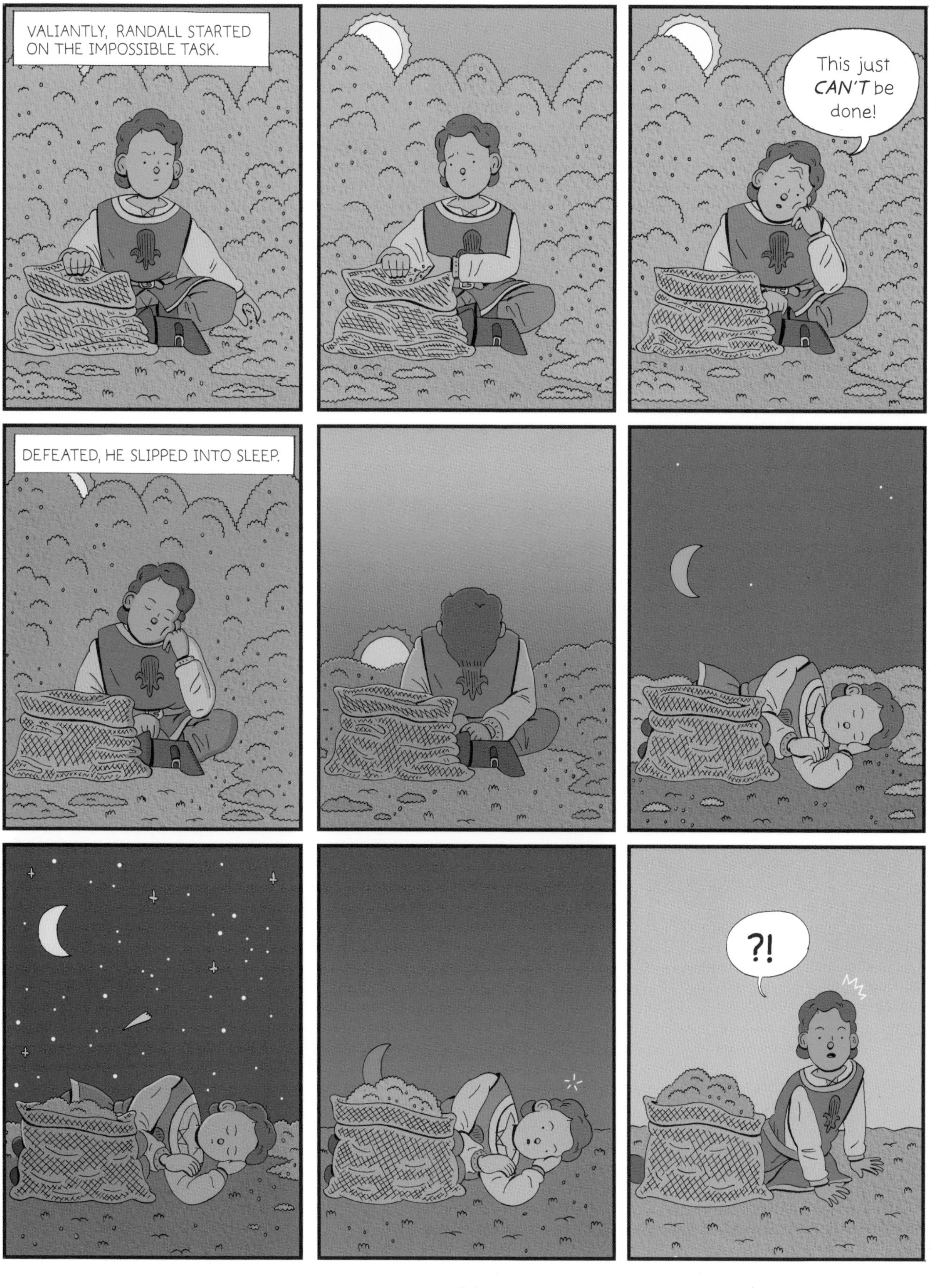
VALIANTLY, RANDALL STARTED ON THE IMPOSSIBLE TASK.
This just CAN'T be done!
DEFEATED, HE SLIPPED INTO SLEEP.
?!

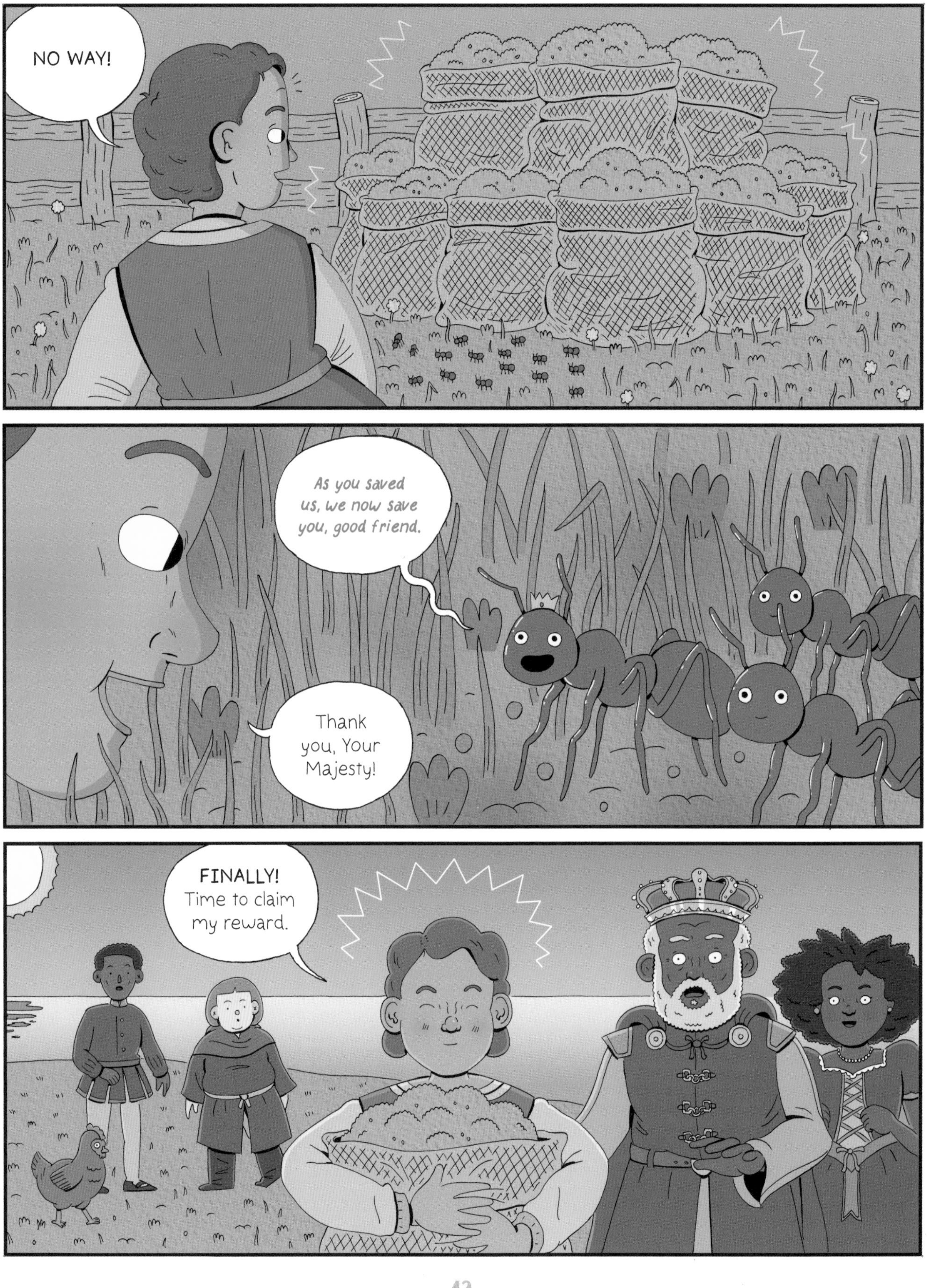
NO WAY!
As you saved us, we now save you, good friend.
Thank you, Your Majesty!
FINALLY! Time to claim my reward.

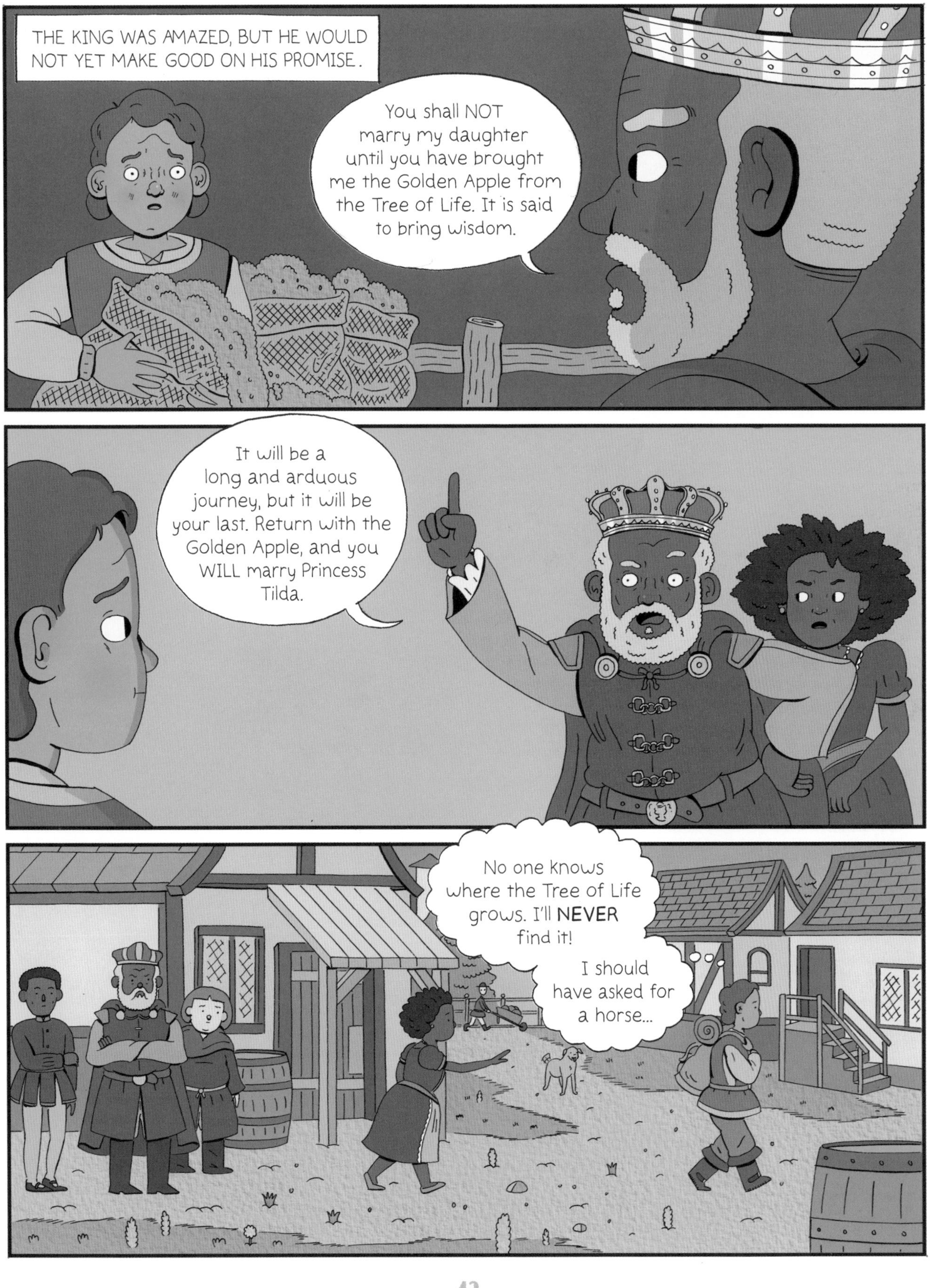
THE KING WAS AMAZED, BUT HE WOULD NOT YET MAKE GOOD ON HIS PROMISE.
You shall NOT marry my daughter until you have brought me the Golden Apple from the Tree of Life. It is said to bring wisdom.
It will be a long and arduous journey, but it will be your last. Return with the Golden Apple, and you WILL marry Princess Tilda.
No one knows where the Tree of Life grows. I'll **NEVER** find it!
I should have asked for a horse...

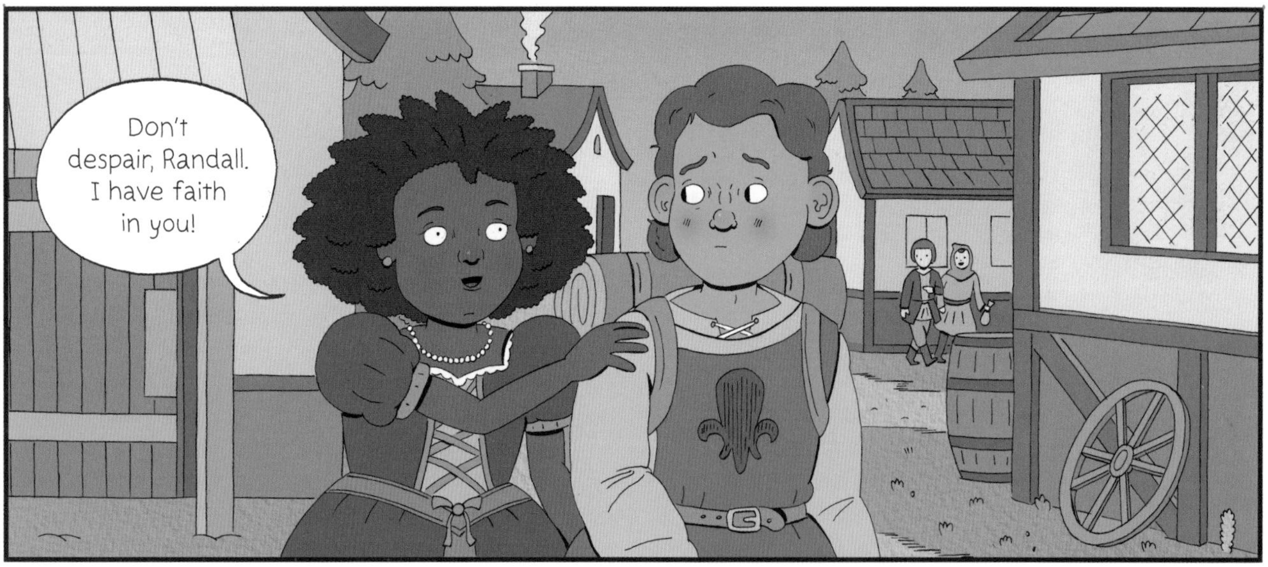
Don't despair, Randall. I have faith in you!

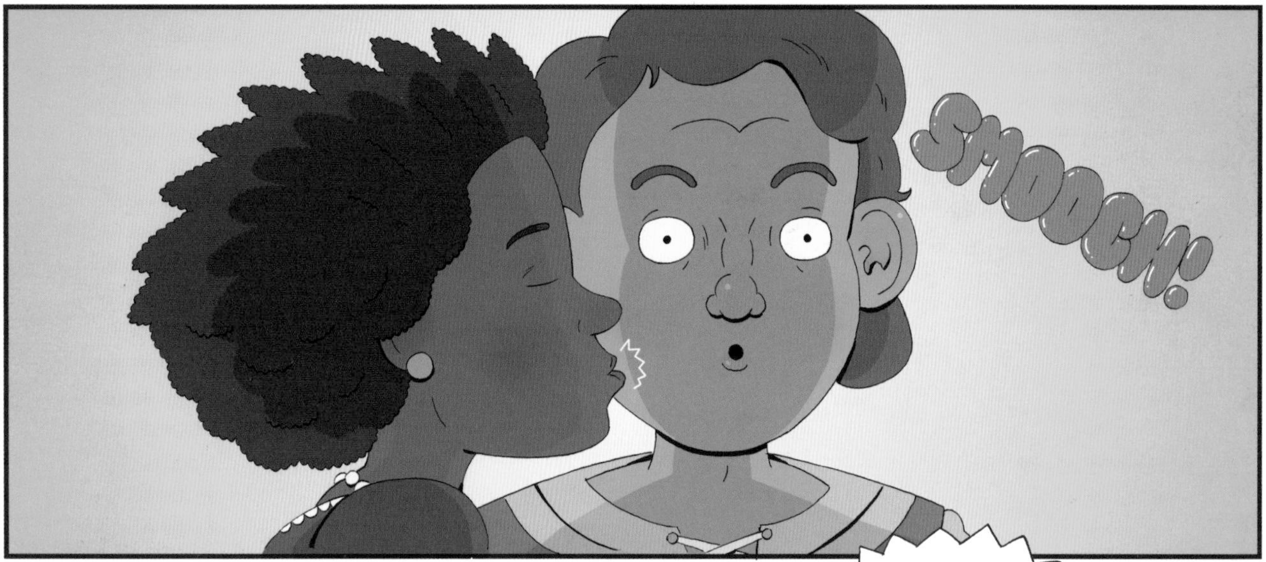
SMOOCH!

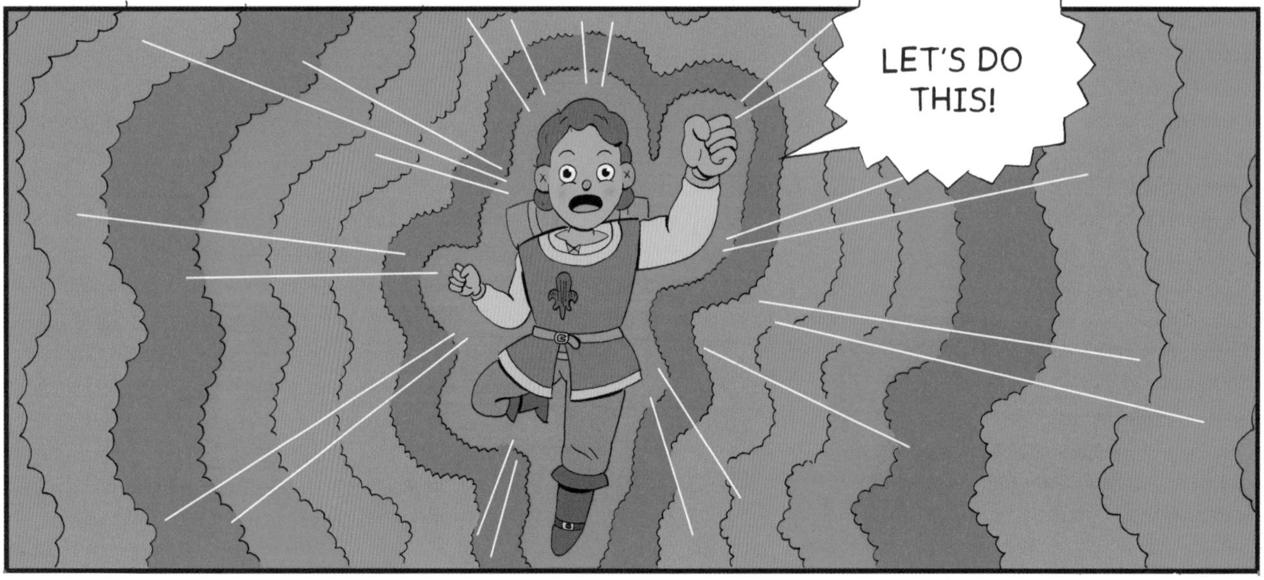
LET'S DO THIS!

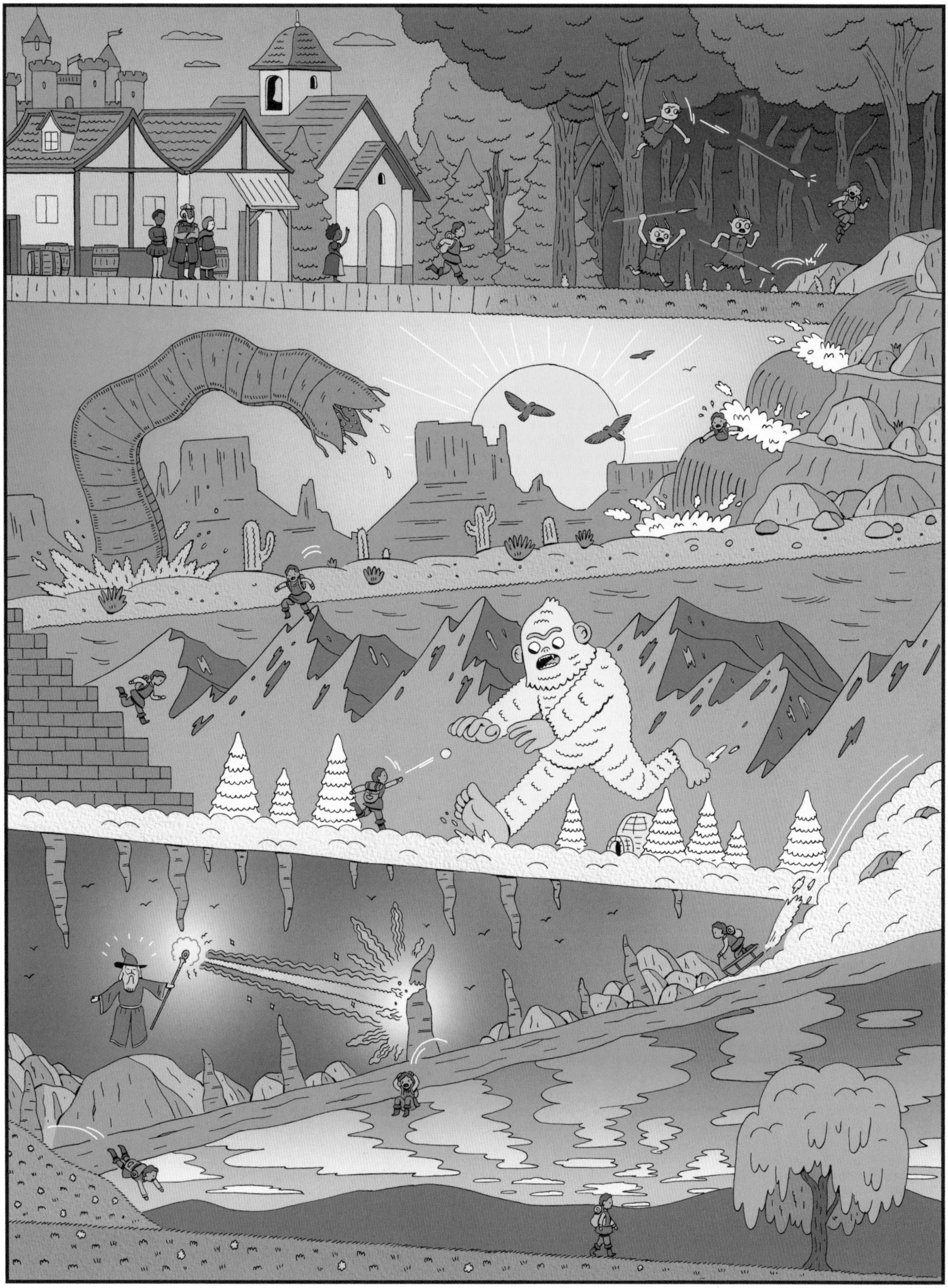

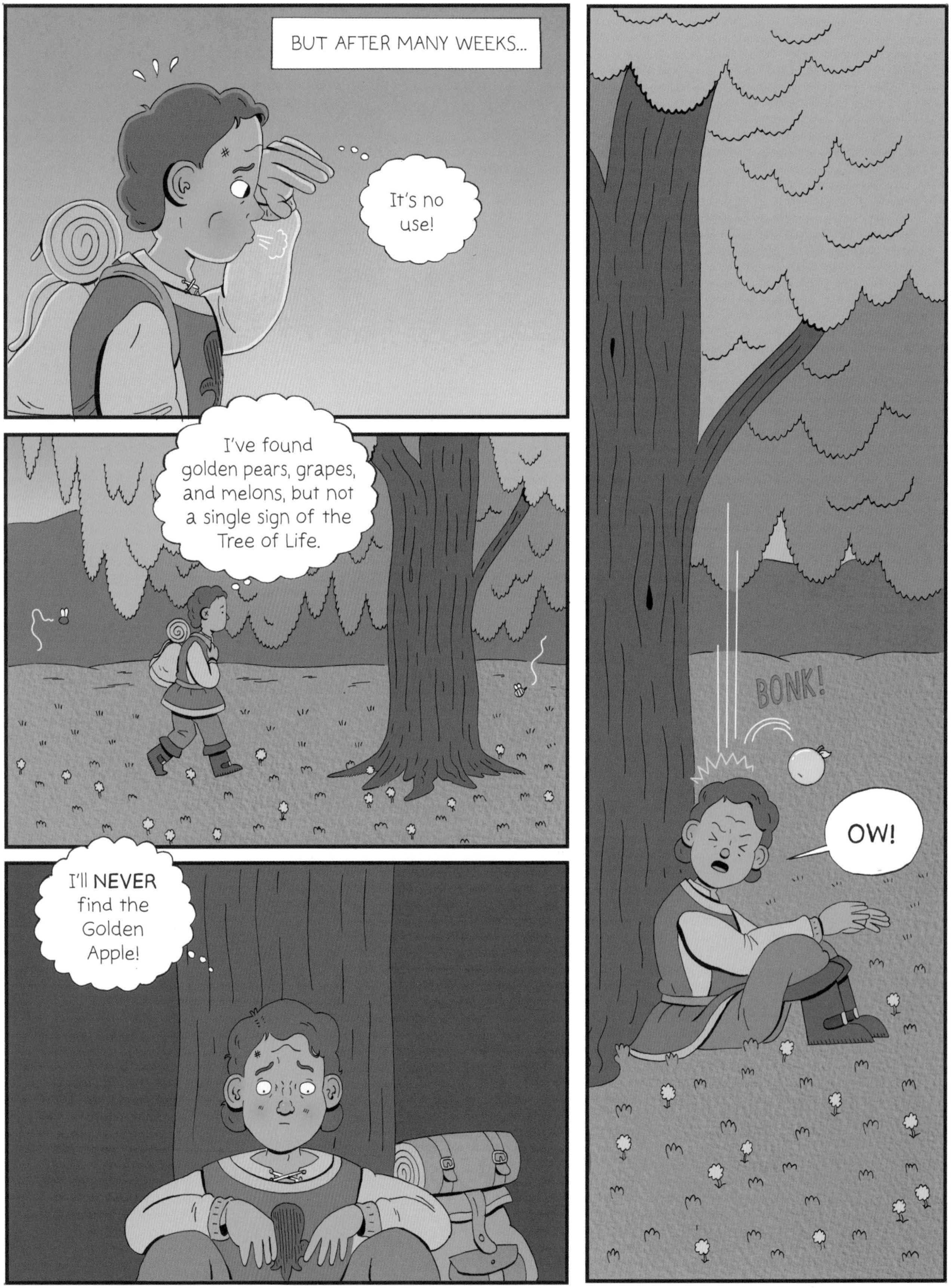
BUT AFTER MANY WEEKS...
It's no use!
I've found golden pears, grapes, and melons, but not a single sign of the Tree of Life.
I'll NEVER find the Golden Apple!
BONK!
OW!

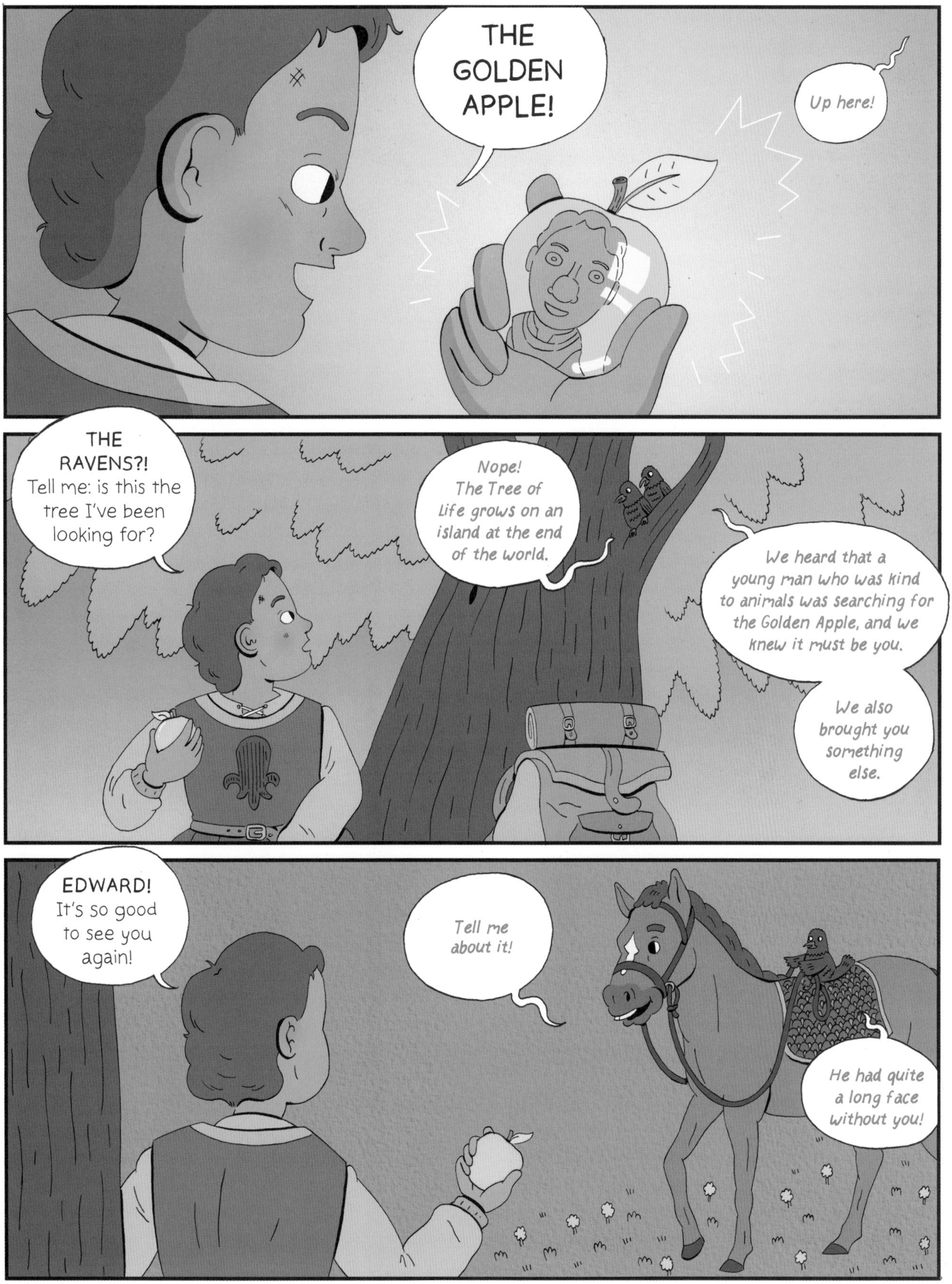
THE GOLDEN APPLE!
Up here!
THE RAVENS?! Tell me: is this the tree I've been looking for?
Nope! The Tree of Life grows on an island at the end of the world.
We heard that a young man who was kind to animals was searching for the Golden Apple, and we knew it must be you.
We also brought you something else.
EDWARD! It's so good to see you again!
Tell me about it!
He had quite a long face without you!

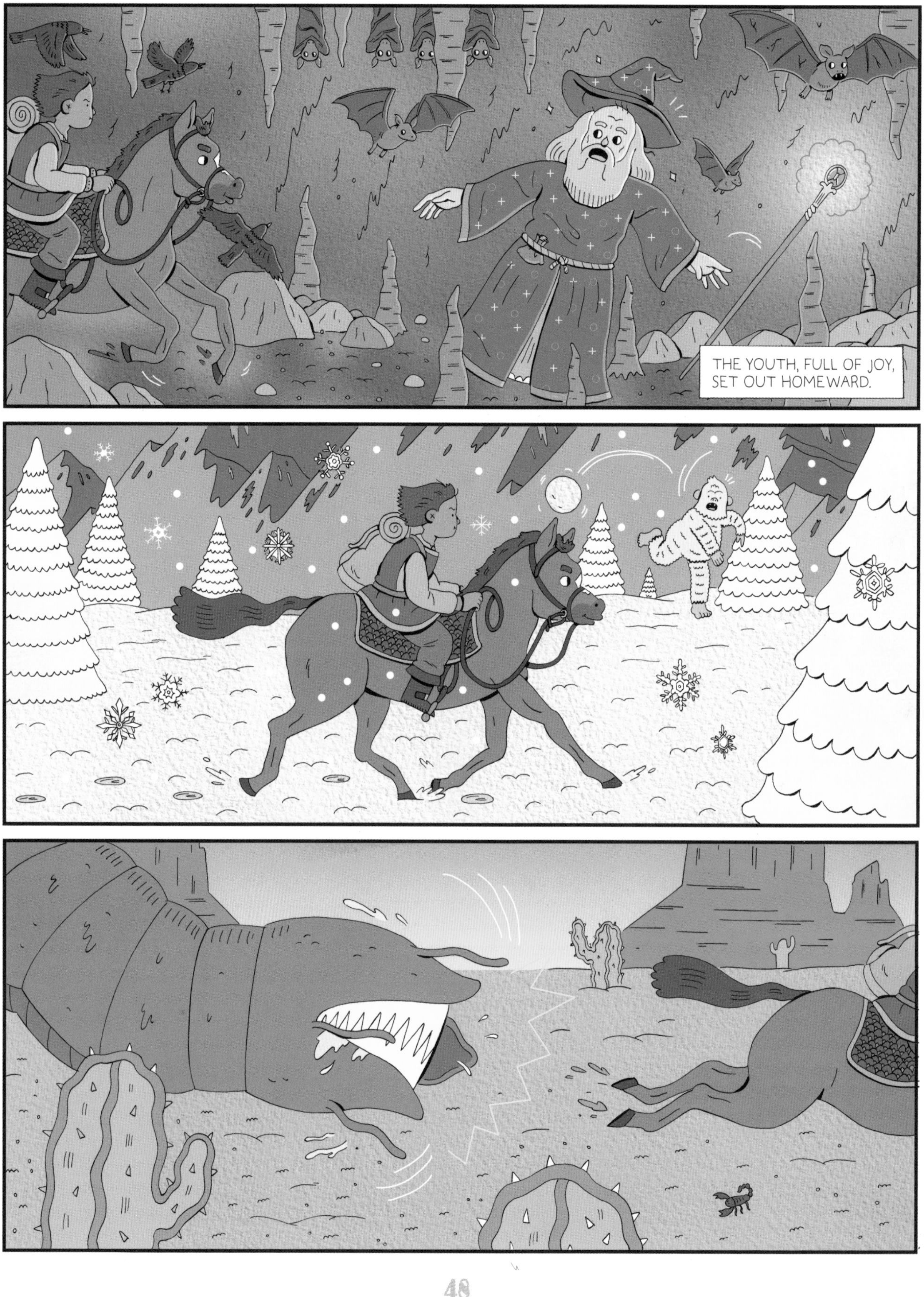
THE YOUTH, FULL OF JOY,
SET OUT HOMEWARD.

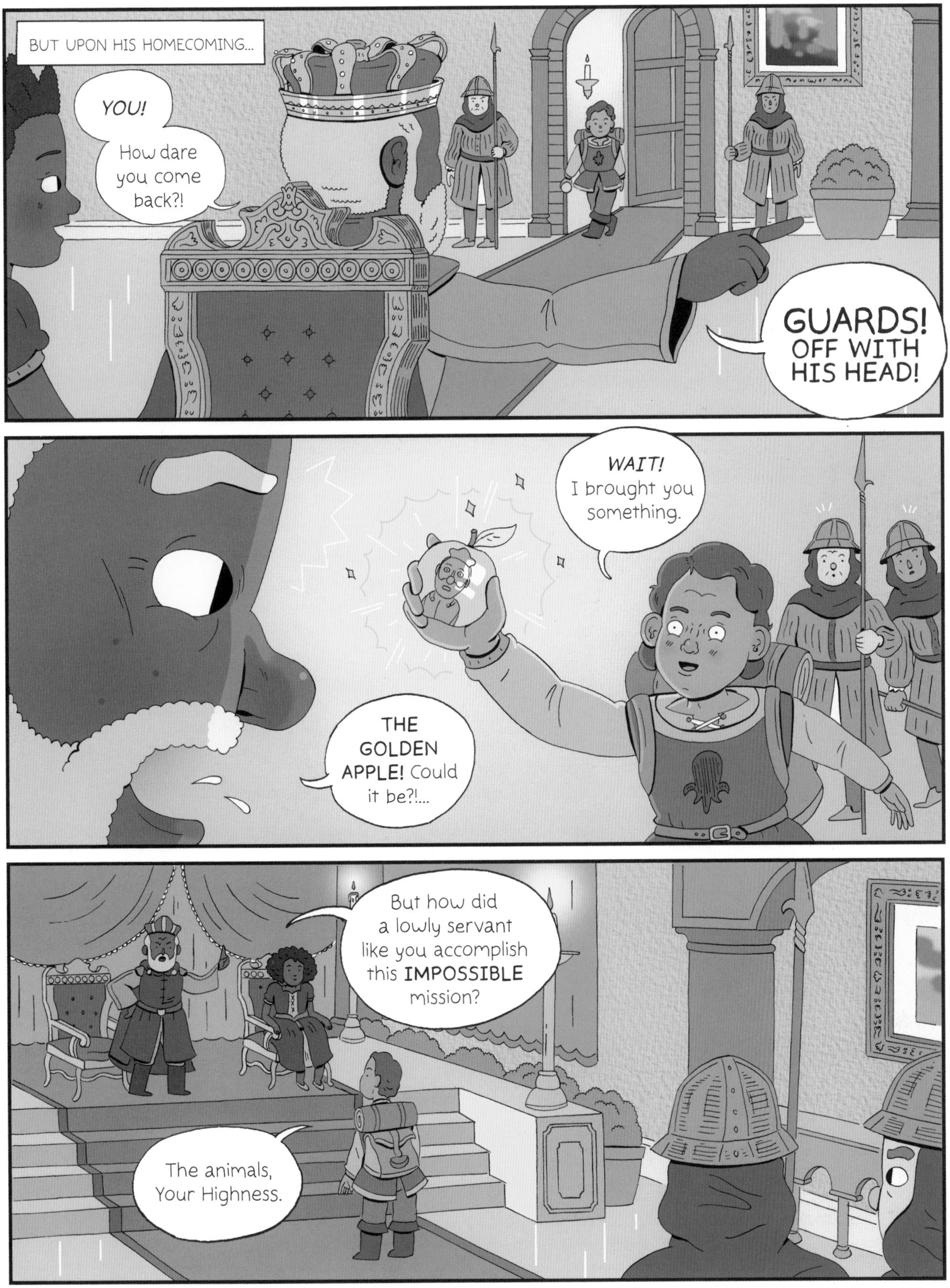
BUT UPON HIS HOMECOMING...
YOU! How dare you come back?!
GUARDS! OFF WITH HIS HEAD!
WAIT! I brought you something.
THE GOLDEN APPLE! Could it be?!...
But how did a lowly servant like you accomplish this IMPOSSIBLE mission?
The animals, Your Highness.

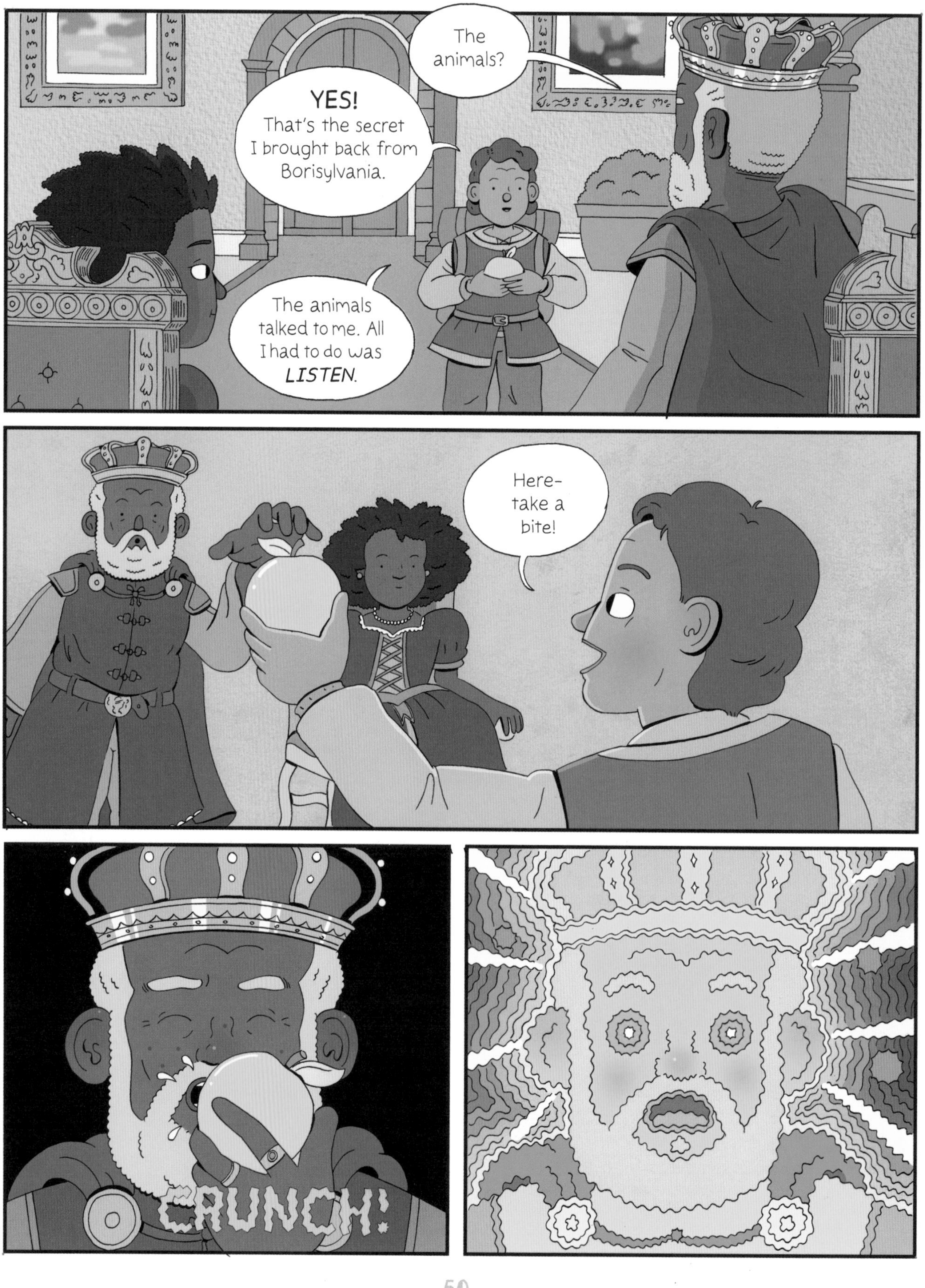
The animals?
YES! That's the secret I brought back from Borisylvania.
The animals talked to me. All I had to do was *LISTEN*.
Here- take a bite!
CRUNCH!

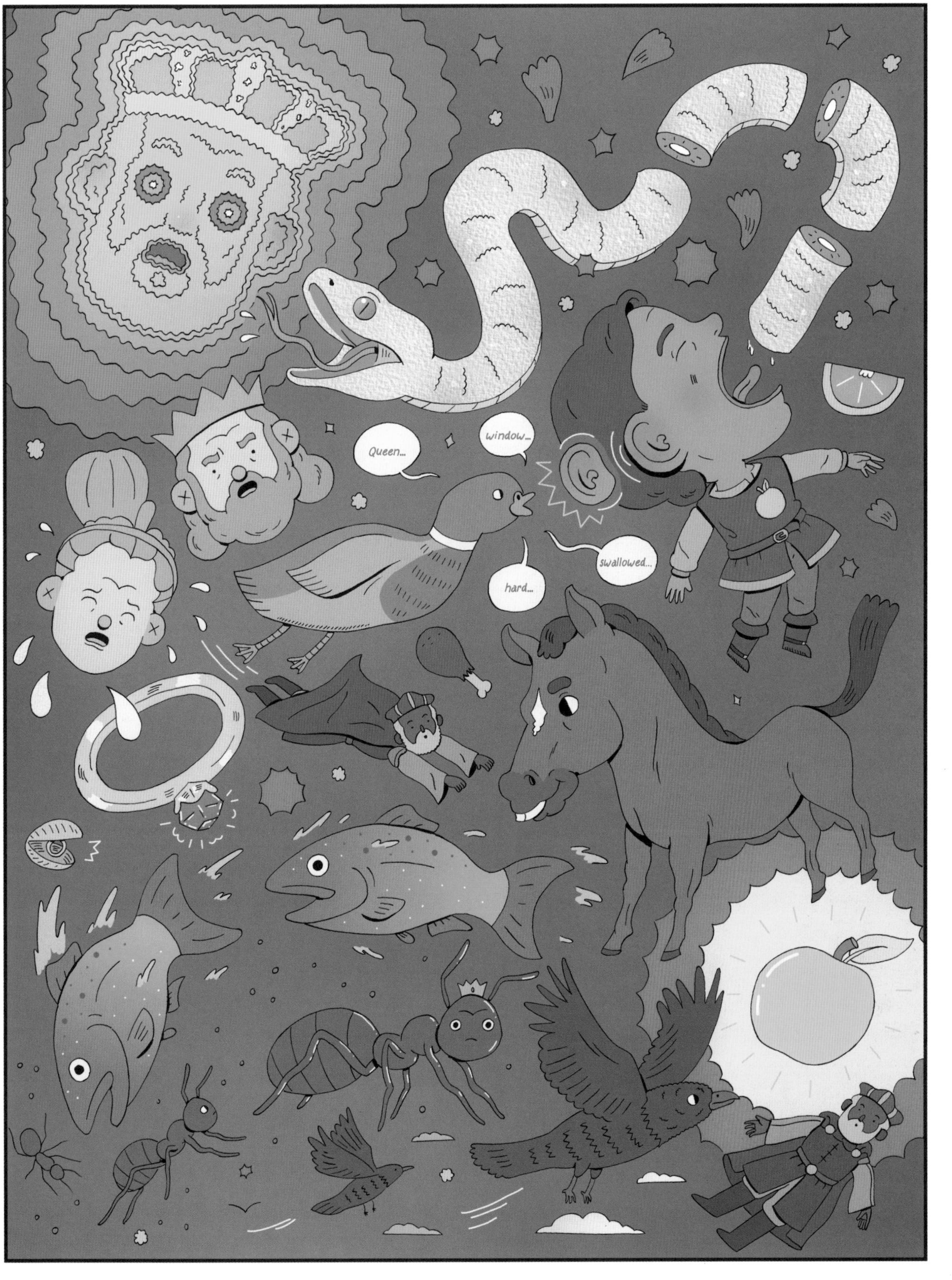
Queen...
window...
hard...
swallowed...

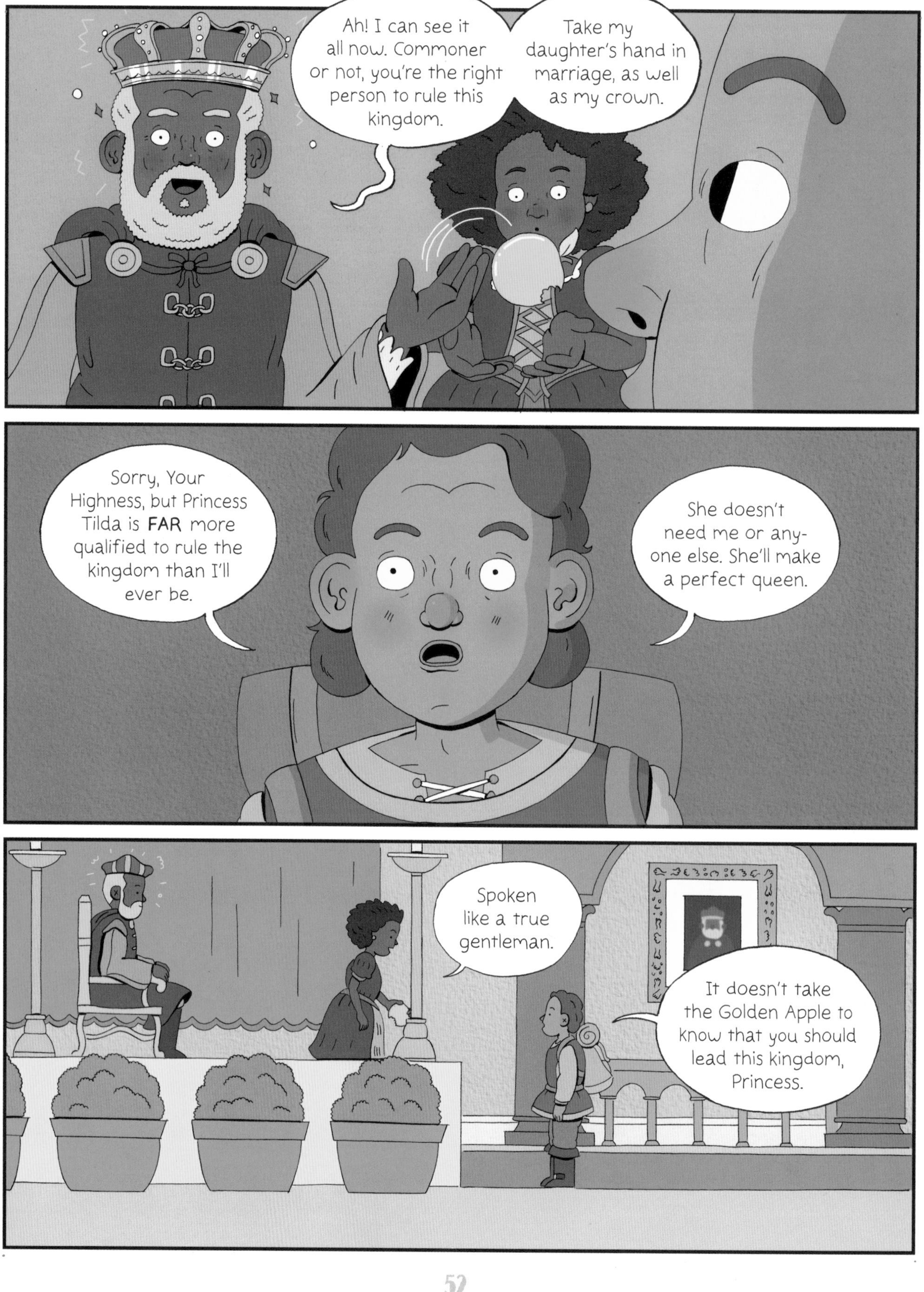
Ah! I can see it all now. Commoner or not, you're the right person to rule this kingdom.
Take my daughter's hand in marriage, as well as my crown.
Sorry, Your Highness, but Princess Tilda is **FAR** more qualified to rule the kingdom than I'll ever be.
She doesn't need me or any-one else. She'll make a perfect queen.
Spoken like a true gentleman.
It doesn't take the Golden Apple to know that you should lead this kingdom, Princess.

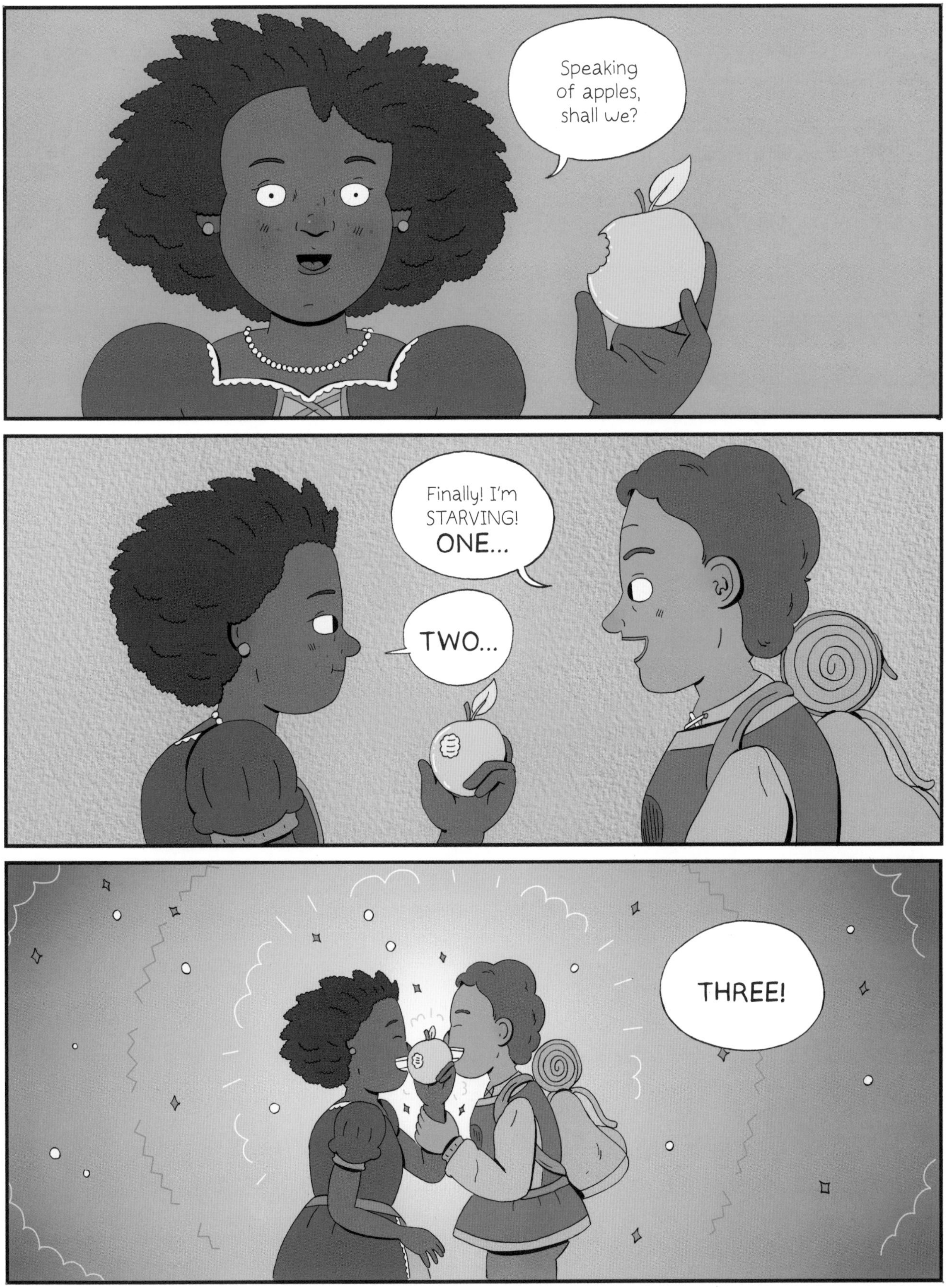
Speaking of apples, shall we?
Finally! I'm STARVING! ONE...
TWO...
THREE!

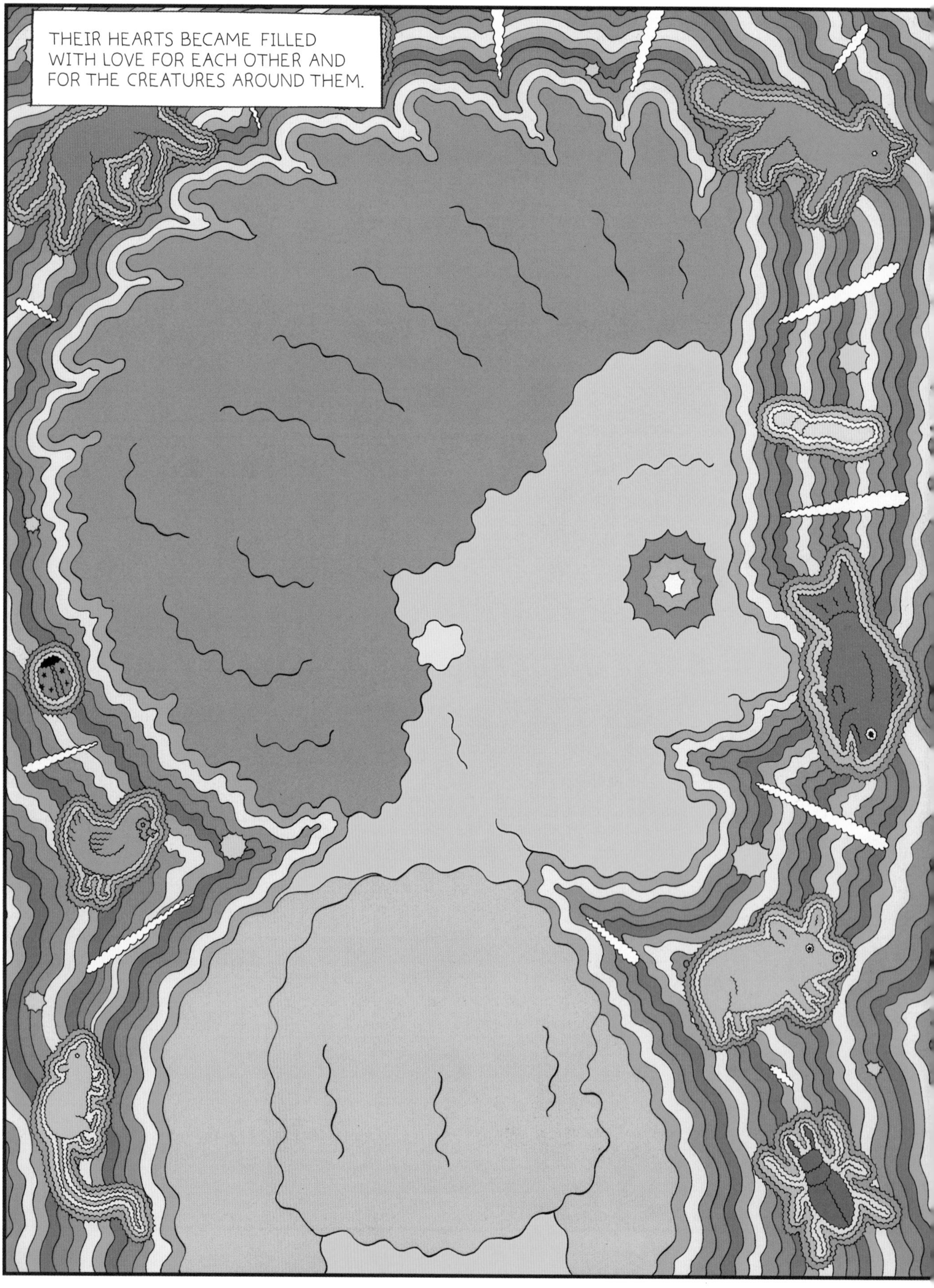
THEIR HEARTS BECAME FILLED WITH LOVE FOR EACH OTHER AND FOR THE CREATURES AROUND THEM.

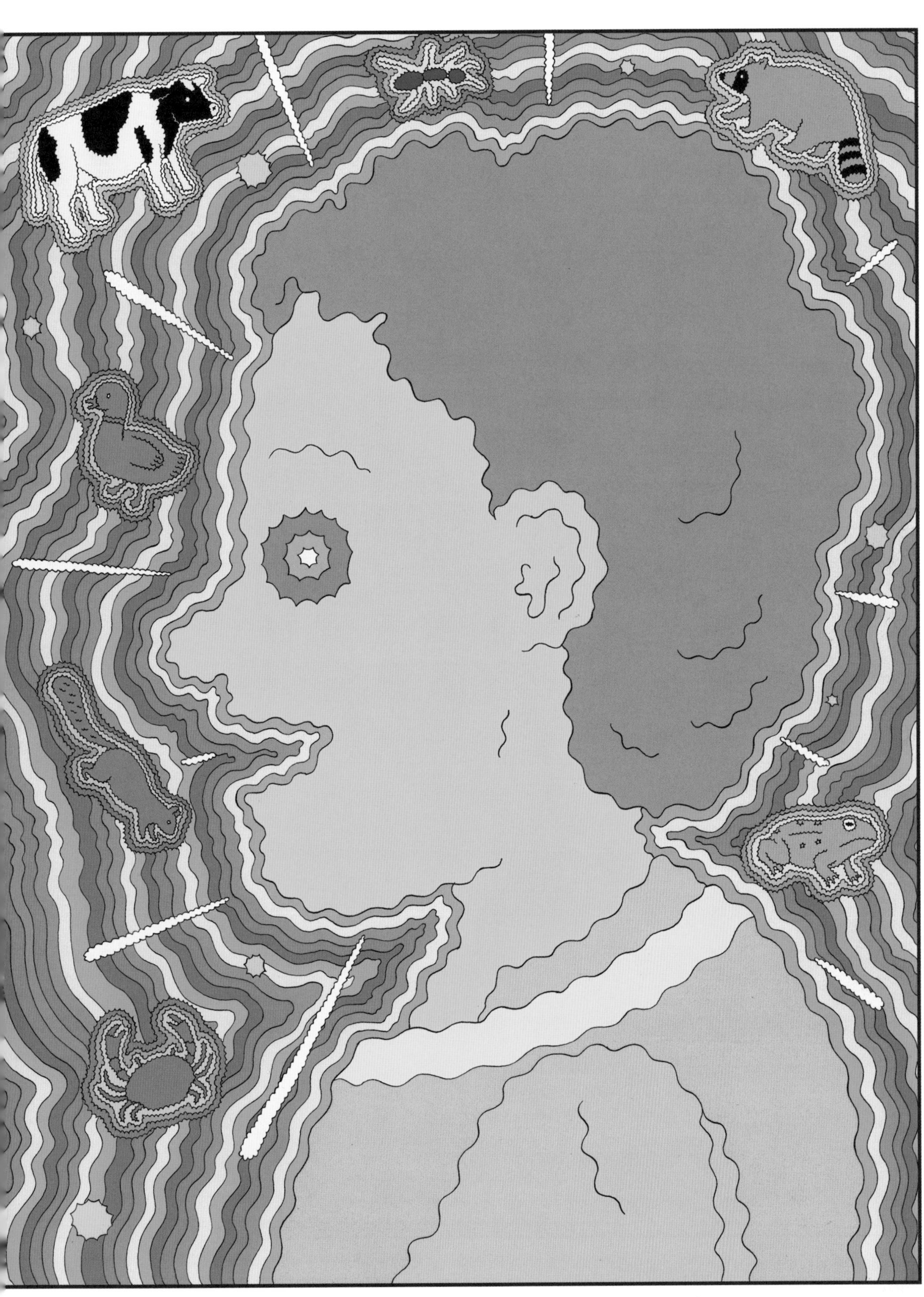

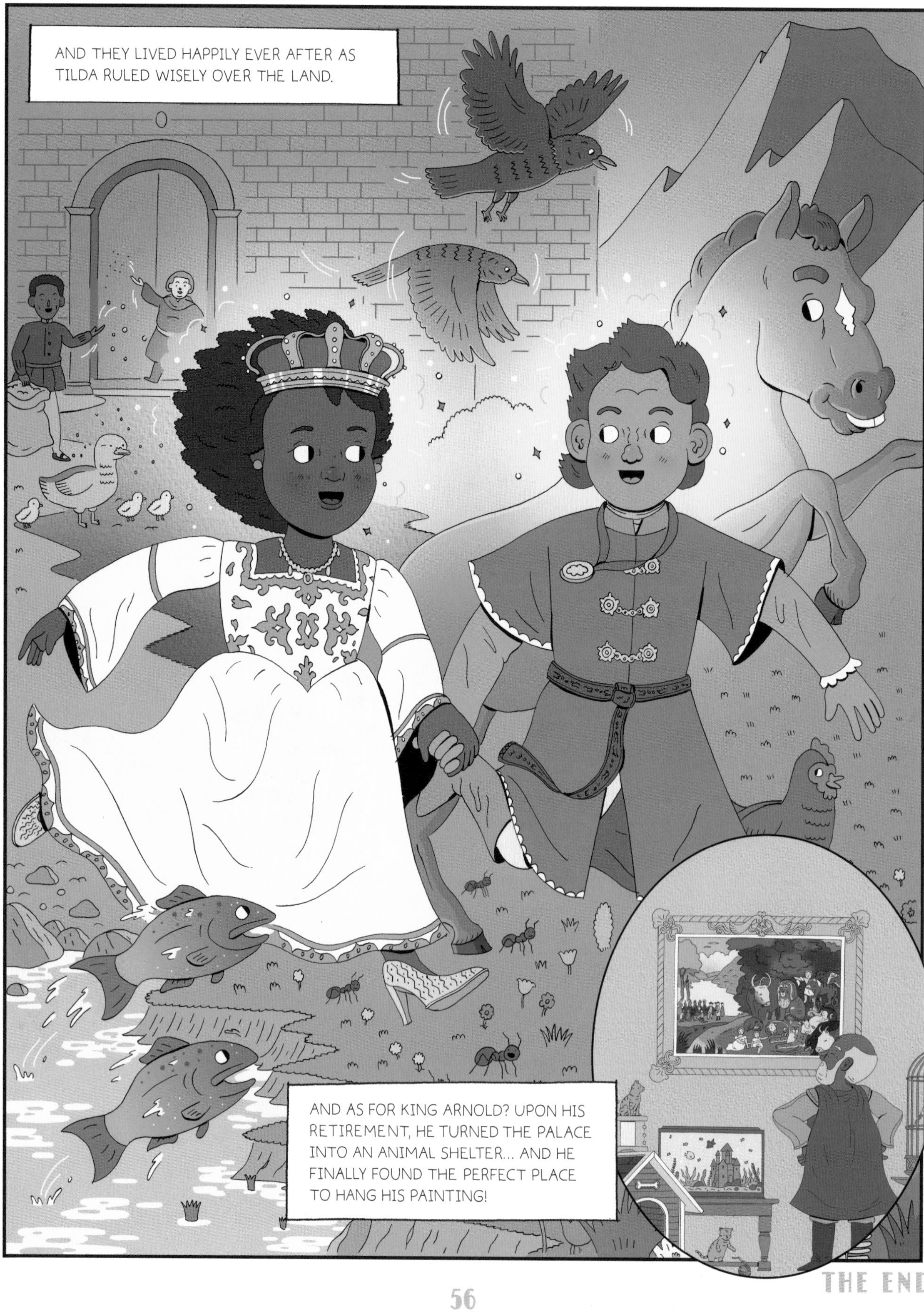
AND THEY LIVED HAPPILY EVER AFTER AS TILDA RULED WISELY OVER THE LAND.
AND AS FOR KING ARNOLD? UPON HIS RETIREMENT, HE TURNED THE PALACE INTO AN ANIMAL SHELTER... AND HE FINALLY FOUND THE PERFECT PLACE TO HANG HIS PAINTING!

THE END

# FOLKTALES: TOLD AND RETOLD

by Paul Karasik

HOUSEHOLD
STORIES,
FROM
THE COLLECTION OF THE BROS:
GRIMM:
TRANSLATED FROM THE GERMAN
BY
LUCY · CRANE;
AND
DONE INTO PICTURES
BY
WALTER · CRANE.
AVENEL BOOKS
NEW YORK

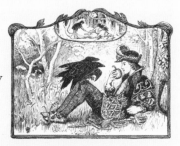

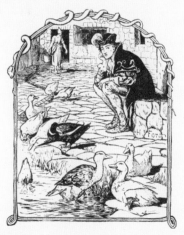

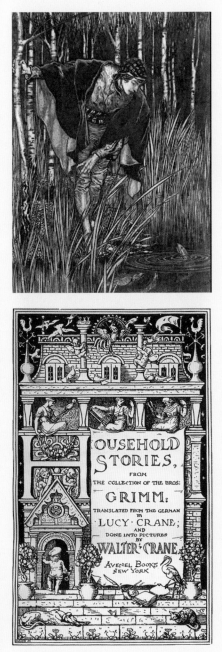

*Clockwise from top left:* Arthur Rackham illustration for a 1916 edition of the Grimms' tales; two of H. J. Ford's illustrations for the 1906 edition of *The Green Fairy Book*, edited by Andrew Lang; title page of the 1920 edition translated by Lucy Crane and "done into pictures" by her brother, Walter Crane.

"The White Snake" appeared in the first edition of the German fairy and folk tales collected by Jacob and Wilhelm Grimm in 1812. The Brothers Grimm, educated at the University of Marburg, set out to preserve what they believed to be the genuine spirit of the German people by collecting the nation's folklore for future generations of scholars. Just as the Grimms' mission was to translate the stories from an oral tradition to a written tradition, cartoonist Ben Nadler has sought to tell the story in his medium, comics. This re-visioning is profoundly a part of the folktale tradition. Folktales are told and retold – and change. Over time, some aspects of a given tale stick, and others fall away. In the case of the Grimms, they culled their tales from storytellers, often women, who had themselves heard them from peasants. Folktales have no distinct authors but are the collective creation of generations of tellers, which makes them all the richer. As the novelist Italo Calvino said, quoting a Tuscan proverb, "The tale is not beautiful if nothing is added to it." And since they have no single author, there are no definitive versions of folktales. There are multiple versions – making it possible, in 1893, for Marian Roalfe Cox to compile three hundred and forty-five different tellings of "Cinderella." There are even varied tellings in the different editions of Grimm. After their initial success, the Grimms began to adapt the stories for an audience that included both scholars and children. All of this is to say that, although rightfully beloved, the Grimms' written versions are far from the "originals" – if such a thing could even exist.

## WHAT IS DIFFERENT IN THIS MODERN RETELLING?

Just as many authors have retold and reconfigured the tales to suit their times and audiences, this volume is no exception. Depictions of gender roles, power, class, authority, and violence in the Grimms' tales reflect a different century. Our version of "The White Snake" continues that tradition of interpretation, adaptation, and re-visioning, including:

"Girl Power!": In the Grimms' version, the king's daughter is a shallow character. She's looking for a husband but cannot see the servant's virtues because of her proud heart. Our princess has the vision to see something special in Randall and the strength and intelligence to eventually inherit and rule the kingdom.

"A rose by any other name would smell as sweet:" "The servant" and "the king's daughter," nameless for the Grimms, were given the names Tilda

and Randall by our cartoonist. Even the horse got a name: Edward.

"My kingdom for a horse!": Randall slays his horse to feed the fledgling ravens in the Grimms' telling, a memorable if gruesome detail. Here, the horse takes care of the raven babies until they learn to fly. The horse has also been given an engaging character, making the reader welcome him back when he reappears towards the conclusion.

"Long Live the Queen!": In the Grimms' story, the monarch of the ants is a king. We now know that ant colonies are, in fact, organized around their queens.

"Peace be with you!": Our version ends with the revelation that the painting that the king has been fretting over during the story is *The Peaceable Kingdom*, by Edward Hicks, a 19th-century American artist. Hicks was so devoted to the idea of all creatures living in harmony that he painted sixty-two versions of that scene.

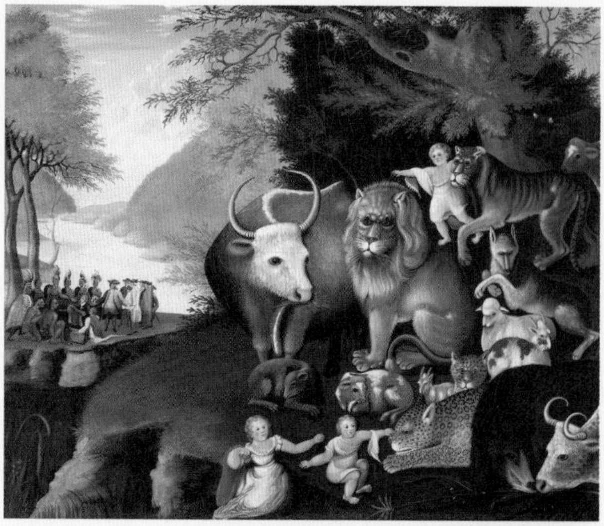

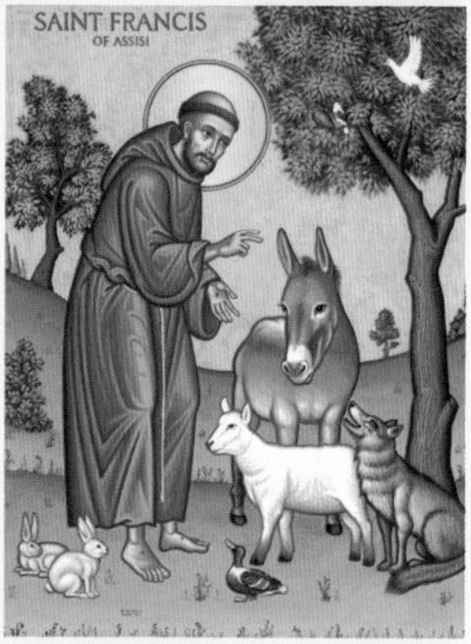
SAINT FRANCIS
OF ASSISI

"What's the big idea?!": Fairy tales are rarely interested in the motives behind the characters' thoughts or actions. The new first act, before the revelation of the contents of the dish, encourages readers to care. By the time the snake dinner is introduced, the reader already sympathizes with Randall and hopes for his success.

## WHAT IS THE SAME IN THIS MODERN RETELLING?

The core of a folktale endures through its many retellings. At the center of this tale are the talking animals. Over the centuries, and in tales from around the world, there are many animal helpers or tricksters, such as Coyote in Native American folklore, Anansi the spider from Africa, Brer Rabbit from the African American traditions, and the European Puss In Boots. A Chinese folktale called "The Legend of the White Snake" tells of an immortal white snake spirit able to turn into a woman.

Often, snakes in folktales behave like ... snakes, treacherous and evil. In Aesop's "The Farmer and the Viper," for example, a farmer rescues a frozen snake which then attacks him, giving rise to the idiom "to nourish a viper in one's bosom" (not a good idea!). Just as treacherous is the snake in the Bible, who gives Eve some very bad advice about an apple from a special tree. Though it also features a couple, a snake, and an apple from an exalted tree, "The White Snake" tells a different story. (This animal role reversal would have been obvious to the Grimms' original audience: the Bible is the all-time best-selling book in Germany – and the second is Grimms'.)

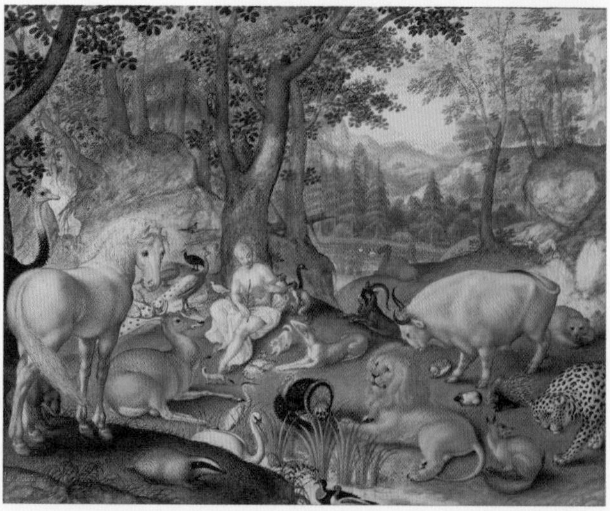

*Top to bottom: The Peaceable Kingdom*, by Edward Hicks, 1826, in the National Gallery of Art, Washington, D.C.; A printed card of Saint Francis talking to birds and animals; *Orpheus Charming the Animals*, by Jacob Hoefnagel, 1613, in the Morgan Library & Museum in New York City.

The ancestor of a tale in which an encounter with a snake leads to wisdom – not death – might be in Greek mythology. In the tale of Melampus, a soothsayer gets his power by helping snakes and in return is given the ability to heal. Similarly, the king in "The Language of Animals," one of the ancient Jātaka tales from India, or the shepherd in "A Snake's Gift," a Serbian tale, acquire their ability to understand the speech of animals, "even ants," after

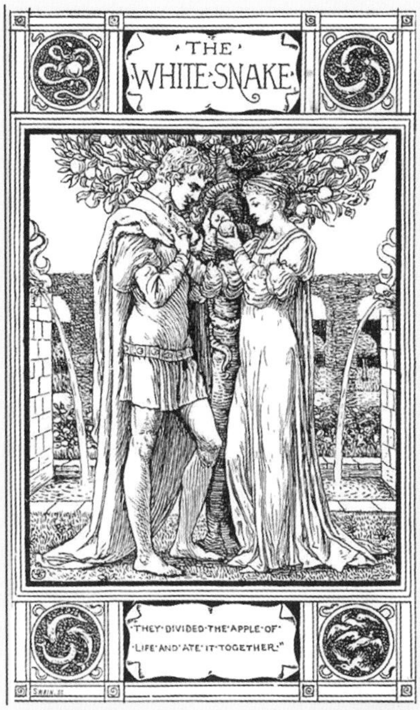
THE WHITE SNAKE
THEY DIVIDED THE APPLE OF LIFE AND ATE IT TOGETHER.

rescuing snakes. (Harry Potter appears to have been born able to understand the snake language of Parseltongue.)

And while traditional tales include people communicating with animals, such as Orpheus charming creatures with his lyre and St. Francis speaking to the birds, few have humans listening to them. This story is built on the idea that nature should be respected, literally listened to, for man to move harmoniously through the world. "I liked the challenge of drawing lowly creatures such ants or fish as intelligent and sympathetic," says cartoonist Ben Nadler. He sums it up neatly: "For me, the takeaway of this tale is simple: stay in tune with nature. Pay attention to the Earth."

Randall is sensitive, listens well, is curious – and is in touch with the natural world. Yet his greatest asset may be his kindness. One by one, his selfless acts towards the animals in the first half of the story are returned in the second half – aiding Randall in his quest. The seesawing cause-and-effect story arc is one of the great pleasures of reading any version of "The White Snake."

## YOUR VERSION OF THE TALE

***New tasks for Randall***: Instead of a fish helping Randall locate a pearl, what kind of task might the king require that, say, a beaver might help out with? Imagine a retelling of this story with a different set of animal helpers.

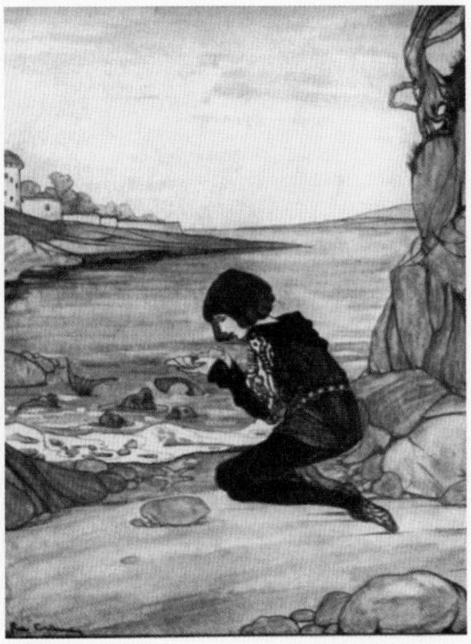

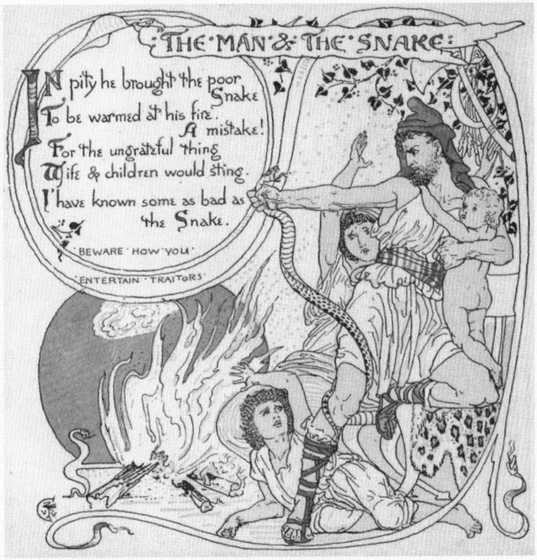
THE MAN & THE SNAKE
In pity he brought the poor Snake
To be warmed at his fire.
A mistake!
For the ungrateful thing
Wife & children would sting.
I have known some as bad as the Snake.
BEWARE HOW YOU ENTERTAIN TRAITORS

*Clockwise from top:* Full-page illustration in the 1920 edition of the Grimms' tales, translated by Lucy Crane and illustrated by her brother, Walter Crane. Crane also illustrated Aesop's fable, "The Farmer and the Viper," (versified by W. J. Linton as "The Man and the Snake"), in *Baby's Own Aesop*, first published in 1887. *Far left:* Illustration by Dutch illustrator Rie (Marie) Cramer for the 1927 edition of the Grimms' tales.

## BIBLIOGRAPHY

*The Annotated Brothers Grimm,* edited by Maria Tatar, Norton, 2012. *New Bicentennial edition of an edition praised for its expert annotations. Ages 8 and up.*

*The Fairy Tales of the Brothers Grimm,* edited by Noel Daniel, Taschen, 2017. *Vintage illustrations highlight how the stories have changed through time. Ages 8 and up.*

*The Original Folk and Fairy Tales of the Brothers Grimm: The Complete First Edition,* Jack Zipes (Translator), Andrea Dezsö (Illustrator), Princeton University Press, 2014. *Gorgeously illustrated, this is the first English translation of the original telling of Grimms' tales. Ages 10 and up.*

*Hansel & Gretel,* Neil Gaiman and Lorenzo Mattotti, TOON Graphics, 2014. *A re-interpretation by Gaiman to match Mattotti's stark black-and-white drawings. Ages 8 and up.*

*The Serpent's Tale: Snakes in Folklore and Literature,* Gregory McNamee (Editor), University of Georgia Press, 2000. *Ages 10 and up.*

*A Tale Dark & Grimm, In a Glass Grimmly,* and *The Grimm Conclusion,* Adam Gidwitz, Puffin Books, 2010-2014. *Child-friendly mix of blood, gore, and black humor by a former teacher. Ages 8 and up.*

**Online Resources:**

HTTPS://ETC.USF.EDU/LIT2GO/175/GRIMMS-FAIRY-TALES/3105/THE-WHITE-SNAKE/
*A free online collection of the Grimm's tales, including MP3 (audiobook) format.*

WWW.PITT.EDU/~DASH/FOLKTEXTS.HTML
*Offers a variety of folklore and mythology texts, arranged in groups of closely related stories.*

WWW.SURLALUNEFAIRYTALES.COM
*Over 1600 annotated folktales and fairy tales.*

WWW.STORIESTOGROWBY.ORG
*Folk & fairy tales from around the world.*

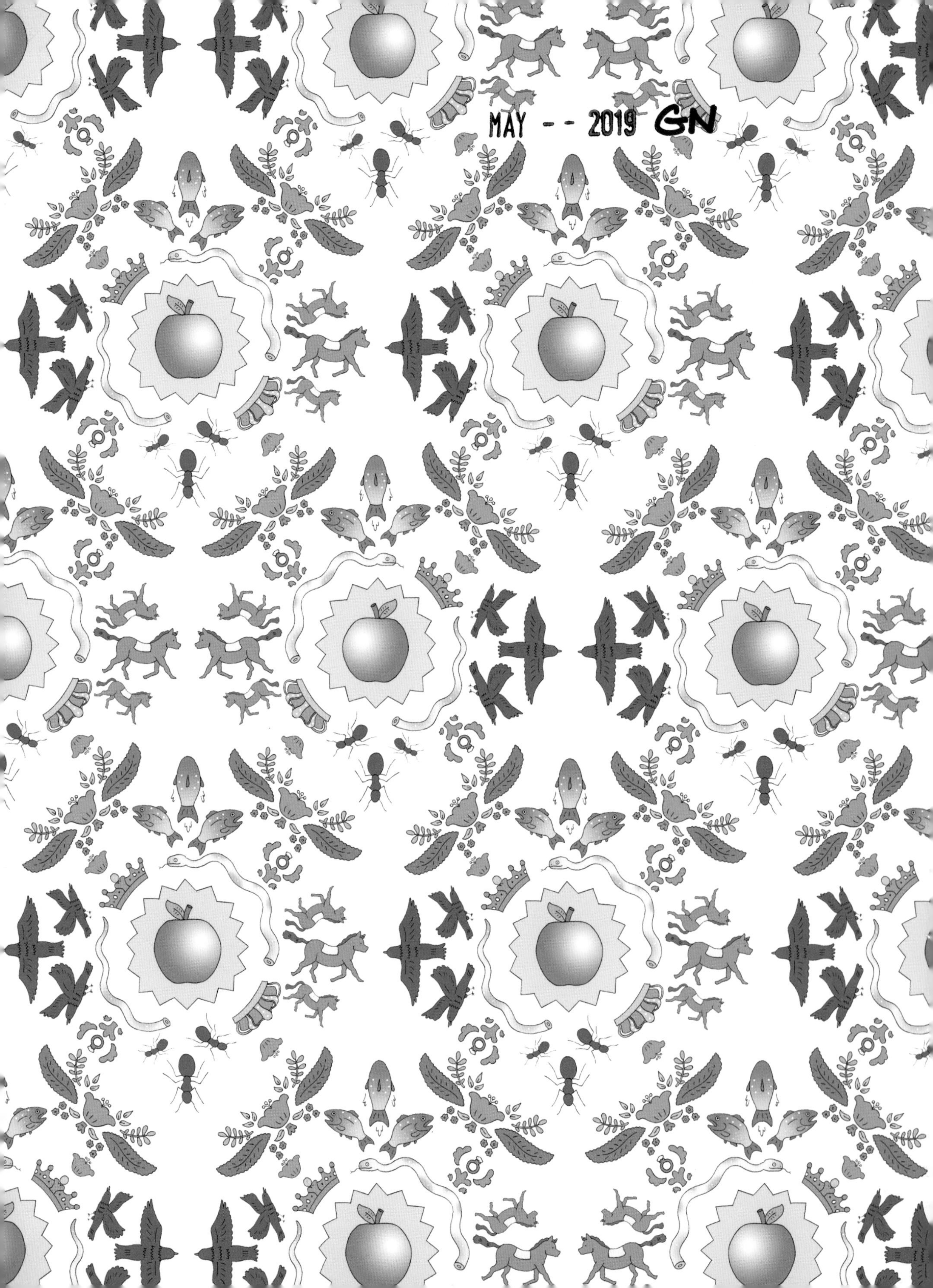